LUDIE'S SONG

In her thirteenth summer Marty suddenly starts to ask questions her mother and father, Uncle Ray and Aunt Letta, haven't got answers for. Why *does* that tearful little boy have to drink from a fountain labeled "Colored"? And why is everyone warning Marty that at her age it's dangerous to remain friendly with the Black children she has always known—just when a secret, forbidden friendship is changing her life?

"The cruel, angry small-town climate is well-realized here. . . . A strong, authentic statement."   —*Kirkus Reviews*

LUDIE'S SONG

LUDIE'S SONG

DIRLIE HERLIHY

PUFFIN BOOKS

PUFFIN BOOKS
A Division of Penguin Books USA Inc.
375 Hudson Street, New York, New York 10014
Penguin Books Ltd, 27 Wrights Lane, London W8 5TZ, England
Penguin Books Australia Ltd, Ringwood, Victoria, Australia
Penguin Books Canada Ltd, 2801 John Street, Markham, Ontario, Canada L3R 1B4
Penguin Books (N.Z.) Ltd, 182–190 Wairau Road, Auckland 10, New Zealand

Penguin Books Ltd, Registered Offices: Harmondsworth, Middlesex, England

First published in the United States of America by Dial Books for Young Readers,
a division of Penguin Books USA Inc., 1988
Published in Puffin Books, 1990
3   5   7   9   10   8   6   4   2
Copyright © Dirlie Herlihy, 1988

LIBRARY OF CONGRESS CATALOGING IN PUBLICATION DATA
Herlihy, Dirlie.   Ludie's song / Dirlie Herlihy.   p.   cm.
Summary: In rural Georgia in the 1950's, a young white girl's secret
friendship with a black family exposes them all to unforeseen dangers.
ISBN 0-14-034245-1
[1. Race relations—Fiction.   2. Friendship—Fiction.
3. Prejudices—Fiction.]   I. Title.
[PZ7.H43126Lu   1990]   [Fic]—dc20   89-36939

Printed in the United States of America
Set in Fairfield

To Lauren Bailey Glass

"Listen to that song, and learn it!
Half my kingdom would I give,
As I live,
If by such songs you would earn it!"

Longfellow, *Tales of a Wayside Inn*

LUDIE'S SONG

ONE

Martha Chafin Armstrong rested her head against the doorframe of the car. She liked the feel of the wind against her face as the car sped past the kudzu-covered countryside. The rich, green vine, so common in the South, lay like leafy down over the ravines and embankments along the highway. Marty, as she preferred to be called, often thought it would be great fun to plunge into the lushness of it.

"Martha Chafin! Stick your head in here. That wind's gonna blow every speck of curl out of your hair."

Marty ducked her head inside the car and turned

to look at her mother, whose hands were white knuc-
kled over the steering wheel.

"Mama, this permanent wave will be on my head
when I die. It's as kinky as nigger hair. I don't know
why I had to get one anyway, just to come down here
and be bored in Caldwell."

"Don't be sassy. Your aunt Letta and uncle Ray are
doing Daddy and me a big favor minding you. I don't
know how else we could have gotten away for such a
long time." Mrs. Armstrong patted her blond hair in
the car's mirror. Marty wished she had hair like that
instead of the brown-red kind of her daddy. At least
she had her mother's blue eyes. "Anyway," her mother
continued, "two weeks will go by before you know it."

"Why couldn't Sara just have come and stayed with
me at the house? I wouldn't miss Anna Raye's party,
or filling up my gossip book 'n all." Marty pulled an
auburn-colored corkscrew from her head, cutting her
eyes to watch it spring back.

She felt her mother's eyes boring hot holes in the
side of her head, and she stared harder out the
window.

"And just where do you think Sara would sleep if
she stayed at our house, young lady?"

Oh for Christmas' sakes, thought Marty. She rolled
her eyes upward and answered with exaggerated pa-
tience, "I've got twin beds in my room, Mama."

"What are you talking about? Sara couldn't sleep
at our house at all!"

"Why not?"

"Martha! Sara's a nigrah, in case you haven't noticed." Her mother's eyes, so like her own, were round with exasperation. "For one thing, it would take forever to get her odor out of the house. Don't be silly."

"Why does everybody think colored people smell bad? All Sara ever smells like to me is sweat, which she gets from working around our house."

In her mind Marty could see Sara, her gray uniform dark with perspiration in the center of her back. She was always there when Marty came in from school, pushing the sweeper or hunched over the ironing board, listening to her stories from the radio on the counter. She couldn't remember a time when Sara had not worked for her family. "Mama, how long has Sara worked for us?"

"Let me see. I know it was during the war, about 1942. You were about two years old, maybe three. Anyhow, we've had her ten years or thereabouts. What difference does it make?"

"I don't know," Marty said with a shrug. "It just seems to me she oughta be like one of our family or something."

"Family? Where do you get such crazy notions?" Mrs. Armstrong's lips pressed together as she slid her eyes in the direction of her daughter. "Listen to me. Sara is a wonderful nigrah. She's a good worker and she knows her place, but coloreds do not live, or more importantly, sleep in the same house with white people. It is unnatural and against God's law. Lord, your daddy would have a fit if he could hear you. Now sit up straight and start looking for a place where we can get a Co-Cola."

Marty sighed. It was hopeless. Actually it wasn't that she minded too much being stuck down here for a while, she told herself. In fact when she was younger, she had looked forward to her family's visits to Caldwell. Aunt Letta and Uncle Ray had no children and were always buying her things and letting her go into Uncle Ray's general store and get candy for nothing. Now she was older, and all her friends were back in the city doing interesting things. She decided right then to make up some exciting story to tell when she got back, so they would be jealous. "Oh, beans," she said aloud.

Before long the familiar signs of nearing Caldwell began to appear: the silo of Turner's dairy farm, steely tall against the hot Georgia sky; the rusty strip of road parting the cornfield in front of Miss Pansy's place; and finally the turnoff, more like a wide path, really, from the state highway.

Caldwell, Georgia, was a town of five hundred people. Marty knew because it said so on the white wooden sign they passed each time they came. It wasn't printed on the sign; somebody had just scrawled the information below the name of the town. Uncle Ray and Aunt Letta lived on the main road of Caldwell, seven houses from the town's business section. Magnolia and oak trees had passed a century guarding the houses on that side of the coppery dirt road into Caldwell. Opposite the houses a wide, weedy field sprawled to the graveled state highway, which arched at the end of the main road, then straightened out toward the next town.

Gravel crunched under the tires as the car turned off the highway. Marty breathed in the country smells, the heat of the June air making them strong: the musty dryness of the weeds, and the sour livestock odors contrasting with the tangy sweetness of honey-suckle vines. There was another scent, too, stronger than the others, which Marty had long associated with this place and no other—the pungency of burning hickory.

When her mother had announced she would take her to Caldwell, Marty had immediately recalled that smoky smell, since, as far as she was concerned, it typified the backwardness of the town. She craned her neck now to confirm the smell's source. Curls of smoke twirled lazily above the dark woods to the right of the highway. Sister, Aunt Letta's washwoman, lived back there, beyond the woods, so the young girl had been told. Marty had never ventured across the highway to find out. When she was real little, they had told her about Sister, boiling clothes to whiteness in a big black pot over a fire in the yard. She had been curious then to see such a thing, but as she grew older and wiser, she began to suspect the old Negro woman of black magic. Nobody in this day and time needed a washwoman, especially when they had their own washing machine. Who knows what really goes on back there in those woods? Marty asked herself.

Aunt Letta got up from her rocker on the porch as the car came to a stop in the driveway. "Nothing ever changes down here," Marty muttered with a sigh. Standing by the car she let her eyes take in the white frame house with its high-pitched tin roof. A long porch across its front gave the house the appearance of a haughty, jut-jawed old woman looking disdainfully at the large pecan trees on either side of the front walk. To the right, next to the driveway, was Miss Julia's, an ugly, two-story brick house whose front porch was lost amid a tangle of honeysuckle and morning glory vines. Miss Julia was a reedy old woman, with two fingers missing from her right hand, who had lived next to Marty's aunt forever. Other than providing some slight fascination when she crocheted with her "bad" hand, the only thing Miss Julia had to offer, as far as Marty knew, was her grandson, Thad, who lived with her. Marty wondered if Thad had changed much.

"Well, hey. How y'all doing?" Aunt Letta's plumpness bounced around her as she walked toward them. "I told Ray I bet you'd be here right after dinner. Did you eat anything? Thelma left some food out. Come here, girl. Give your aunt Letta a big hug."

Cloroxed to death, thought Marty as she was enfolded in her aunt's fleshy, bleachy smell. Her cheek nearly dislodged the two wave clips Aunt Letta wore in her hair, since Marty was almost half a head taller than her aunt's four feet eleven inches. The little woman stood back and placed her hands on her hips, calling shrilly to Mrs. Armstrong across the car. "Beth, you can't let this young'un grow another inch. She's gettin' too big now." The round face beamed at Marty. "But you're just as pretty as a picture! Yes ma'am."

Later Marty stood beside Aunt Letta again in the drive, waving good-bye to her mother. When the car turned onto the highway, Aunt Letta put an arm across Marty's shoulder. "Well, sugar pie, let's us go sit on the porch and wait for Uncle Ray."

Marty took her place in the cane-backed rocker next to her aunt and gazed out across the field connecting the road with the state highway. The smoke from Sister's had settled into a blue-gray fog, hovering over the dark tops of the trees. "Sister must be through doing the wash, huh, Aunt Letta?"

Her aunt stretched her neck forward. "Reckon so. Through with the boiling, anyway."

Marty took a deep breath. "Aunt Letta? Why does she wash for you when you have your own washer?" She hoped she hadn't sounded too smart-alecky.

"Well, she just does, that's all. Sister takes care of the flatwork for us, like sheets 'n all. Your uncle Ray believes in helpin' out the nigrahs, so he gives 'em things they can do. He's real good to 'em, but he don't give no charity. No ma'am. Ray believes in the nigrahs keeping their self-respect, doing jobs for pay." Aunt Letta punctuated the last word with a sharp nod of her head, her eyes bright with Christian kindness. The next instant her hand moved to the wave clips and she rose, taking the clips from her hair and slipping them into the pocket of her housedress. "Here comes that ol' truck now, Martha. Your uncle Ray is coming down the road."

TWO

It was the crispness and ironed smell of the pillowcase that awakened Marty the next morning. Raising herself on one elbow she blinked her eyes open to the flowered print of the bedroom curtains. "Mmmmm, Aunt Letta's," she mumbled, falling back against the pillow. From the kitchen her aunt's high-pitched voice could be heard reciting the activities of the day to Thelma, the cook, and occasionally the deeper voice of her uncle Ray.

Her uncle would make the next two weeks tolerable, she had decided last night. A kind of brightness was missing when he wasn't around, she thought, remembering how her spirits had risen yesterday when he came up the front walk. His sandy hair was graying a bit, but his dark eyes still danced as if he had some marvelous secret. Everybody said he was the "spittin' image" of Grandpa Armstrong, but since the old man had died when Marty was an infant, she didn't know about that.

Actually, Uncle Ray was her daddy's half brother, born to her grandfather and his first wife. George, Marty's father, and Lonnie, the youngest brother, were children of a second, much later marriage. Uncle Ray was the only one of the Armstrong boys who had stayed on in Caldwell after the war, and now he practically ran the town. Marty didn't care what her daddy said about his being a "big fish in a little pond"; she liked the way the people in Caldwell looked up to her uncle. He was always thinking up things for her to do, too, even though Aunt Letta said he just liked to show her off, taking her on his rounds to tenant farmers and letting her clerk in the store. He was sure enough her favorite uncle, even if he had beat her at Parcheesi last night.

Suddenly a yowling, half animal, half human, tore at the morning stillness. Marty sat up straight, turning toward the window. The sound grew louder, and Marty felt her heart rock like the night she and Anna Raye had thought the bush on the window was Dracula. Someone, something, was making awful noises, and it seemed closer with each one! Gradually she became aware of her head nodding in rhythm to the wailing outside. "Yanh, yanh, yanh . . . ee . . . ee . . . yanh." It was so loud now that she knew it must be right outside the window. Should she get out of her safe sheet cocoon? Slowly Marty edged to the end of the bed, then dashed quickly to the window, her feet barely touching the cool wooden floor. She crouched beneath the curtains, a warm breeze stirring them in her face. By now the howling was earsplitting, and as she eased the curtain aside to peer into the lane next to the house, Marty felt saliva rise up in her mouth.

Outside in the lane was a hideous young colored woman, the ugliest being Marty had ever seen. She struggled by, dragging one leg, which bent at an angle beneath her faded skirt. A misshapen arm bound a sack to her frail body. Marty stared, transfixed, not daring to look at the girl's face. Then she shuddered and forced her eyes upward. One of the girl's eyes stared straight ahead, and the other was partially covered by a scrap of dark skin that extended like a ghastly appliqué over the side of the creature's face, separating around a mouth that seemed weighted down on one side and that twisted grotesquely with each peculiar sound it made. A bright-blue cloth wrapped the Negro's head, which balanced a cloth-covered basket. When the basket had disappeared around the corner, Marty leaned back against the wall, pulling her seersucker nightgown over her knees. Suddenly she was

very cold. When she was four years old, Uncle Ray
had told her about Soap Sally, an old woman who
boiled up little girls to make soap out of them when
they were bad. As she grew older, she thought how
dumb she had been to be scared of some faceless
phantom. Considering what she had just seen outside
the window, though, anything seemed possible.

Now the eerie whining came from inside the house,
and Marty tiptoed to the door of the bedroom and
cracked it. Aunt Letta's back blocked her view, and
she heard her speak.

"You tell Sister Miss Martha's here, so we'll have
more sheets this week." Then her aunt moved to one
side and Martha had a clear view of the girl leaning
against the refrigerator. Her bent leg angled out from
her body, giving her appearance a kind of casual non-
chalance. It was always hard to determine the age of
a colored person, but Marty guessed the woman, or
girl, to be in her late teens or early twenties. Her
lower jaw moved from side to side as if trying to force
form into the babel she used for communication. Suddenly the Negro was silent, and Marty was sure that
her one eye was fixed on the crack in the bedroom
door. Just before she gently eased the door shut, Marty
saw the girl's crooked mouth stretch to a hideous grin.

"Wait'll I tell Anna Raye I saw an honest-to-good-
ness witch," Marty said softly. As she pulled on her
playsuit, her mind zigzagged from notion to notion
until she remembered she had heard Sister's name.

That's it! This wretched freak was probably the old colored woman's doing. Maybe she had even made her, like—like Frankenstein!

"Ludie?" Marty was combing her hair when she heard her aunt call. "You tell Sister I thank her for the jelly, too, hear?"

When Marty came into the kitchen, she was relieved to find only Thelma.

Thelma was Sara's Caldwell counterpart. Marty knew that each morning she appeared and remained to do the daily cooking and cleaning chores and had done so for many years. Like so many other things in Caldwell, Thelma never changed.

Her body was large boned and lean; her facial features were big too. Marty used to think that Thelma had the biggest face she had ever seen, and that she was probably descended from a race of Amazons Marty had read about in a Wonder Woman comic book. The main difference between the two servants, however, was their personalities. Sara was lighthearted, often singing and chuckling out loud for reasons known only to herself. But not Thelma. She hardly ever smiled, much less laughed.

Marty headed for the electric percolator and opened the cupboard overhead for a cup.

"Dey 'low you drink coffee now, Miss Martha?" asked Thelma.

"Thelma, I'm nearly thirteen years old, for goodness' sakes. Besides, I been drinking it with half milk since I was tee-nincy, and it haddn't turned my feet black yet, like everybody said."

"Das fact, miss'um. Dey ain't black," Thelma said, disappearing into the pantry at the back of the kitchen.

Marty followed and stood in the doorway while Thelma scooped up lard from a can big enough for Marty to hide in.

"Thelma, what's wrong with that colored girl who was in here? Does she live in Caldwell? I never saw her."

"Ludie? You never did see her? Must be 'cause you gen'ly come on Sat'dys, or Sunday, and she mos' always git de wash back fo' then. She Sister's girl. Got burnt when she was half growed." Thelma tapped the lid of the can all around and lumbered past Marty into the kitchen.

"Why can't she talk?" Marty asked Thelma's back.

"Some say powerful lots of smoke from the fire got all in her speakin' parts and burnt 'em up bad."

The back screen snapped shut and Aunt Letta clumped into the kitchen, fanning the heat of the morning air. "I thought I heard you up, Missy. Thad was over here this morning at the crack of dawn wantin' you, but your uncle Ray said we'd let you sleep your first morning. Soon as you're through with your breakfast, I speck you ought to go see him. He said he'd be waiting to pick blackberries if you want to."

"Can Thelma make a pie if I get enough?"

"We'll see, but you just remember you got to wear your oxfords into those snaky bushes, not them sandals you got on."

Marty and her oxfords found Thad sitting on the swing on his grandmother's front porch. "Heyy, Martha," he drawled, eyeing the bucket swinging at her side. "You want to go get some blackberries?"

Marty picked up a Classic Comics lying next to Thad, and a Plastic Man slid to the floor. She bent down to get the book and cocked her head to look up at Thad. He took the comic from her and moved over, making room for her on the swing. "Your bigmama making you read that stuff again this summer?" Marty asked as she sat down.

Miss Julia had taught school in the county for many years and was determined that her grandson would have a proper education. Once when Marty and her parents were in Caldwell, Thad had been unable to play because he had not finished his required reading for the week. On the trip back home she had heard her daddy talking about the Yankee violin player who was Thad's father. He had come to Caldwell one time with Thad's mother and had been overheard to make some remark about ignorant Southerners. Marty's daddy had said he guessed that was why Miss Julia made Thad read so much.

Thad's mother, Naomi, was Miss Julia's only child. She was a singer in opera, Marty thought, but she was never sure of the details. She had heard her sing once at the church in Caldwell, "Open My Eyes that I May See," and it had sounded just like Kathryn Grayson in the movies. Marty wasn't sure just why Thad lived with his bigmama instead of his mother. Aunt Letta had said it was because Naomi traveled all over singing, so she guessed that was why. Anyway he sure looked a lot like her, except his dark hair was always hanging down in his eyes, which were green and too big for his narrow face. Like whoever put him together didn't leave room enough for them.

The big eyes were on her chest now. Her mother was right. She would need a bra soon.

"Well, do you want to? I got me a bucketful day 'fore yesterday over yonder back of town where we went that time."

She felt embarrassed about her chest and folded her arms across it. "Yeah, I guess, but in a minute. Thad, you ever see Ludie, Sister's daughter?"

Thad picked at a wart in the palm of his hand. "Uh-huh. What about her?"

Marty shifted in the swing, and her eyes fastened on a hummingbird burrowing his beak deep inside a morning glory trumpet. "Nothing special, 'cept I think she looks like a witch or something."

"No, she don't. Just looks like a nigger that got burned up."

"Well, Aunt Letta told me how Sister does the wash in those big pots 'n all."

"Uh-huh?" He was looking at the edge of her hair. "How'd your hair get like that?"

Marty heaved her shoulders in exasperation. "Thayad! I was talking about Sister, and doing the washing in those pots. Besides, my mama made me get a permanent and that's why my hair's messed up. Now, but don't you think it's funny for somebody to do wash for people who have their own washing machines? I saw a social studies film about voodoo and headhunters last year? And it showed a bunch of colored natives boiling up animals and putting spells on people, and they were doing it in big black pots. Soon as I saw it, I thought of Sister, and that was before I ever laid eyes on Ludie!"

Thad wagged his head slowly and rolled his eyes in mock disgust. "Marth—Marty, niggers can have all the black pots in their yards they want to. It don't mean they're witchifying or nothing." His eyes flickered to her face, then quickly to the porch floor. "Your aunt Letta told Bigmama you got too much imagination sometimes for your own good," he said softly. Thad rose, picking up the bucket beside the swing. "If we're gonna get back for dinner, we ought to go on."

"Okay, but will you go with me tomorrow after church?"

"Go where?" Thad was walking down the steps and turned to look up at Marty.

"To Ludie and Sister's house. To see, 'n all."

"Ain't no need, but I will if you want to."

Marty stepped from the porch to the brick pillars on the other side of the steps, then jumped to the ground. Boy hidey, as Uncle Ray would say. Was she going to have something to tell when she got back home!

THREE

The sun streaked heat waves through the leaves of the pecan trees, dappling Marty's arms and legs as she passed beneath them on her way to the road that led to town. Uncle Ray had asked her to come to the store and help file charge slips, which had been "piling up mightily" after a busy Saturday morning. Behind her the clang of metal and china from the house as Thelma worked in the kitchen mingled with the *ribble* of her aunt's rocking chair across the front porch. Marty was glad to have something to do besides "rock to China" with Aunt Letta this afternoon.

As she stepped onto the dusty copper road, she

glanced toward Miss Julia's big brick house. Although Thad had been useless in providing any clue to Ludie's "real" identity, he had promised, reluctantly, to go with her to Sister's after church tomorrow. "How in the world people can live with two surefire witches under their noses and not know it is beyond me," she said under her breath.

Saturday mornings were the busiest at Armstrong's General Store, since farmers brought their families into town for haircuts and for groceries they could not get from their land. The whole town had a carnival atmosphere. By the afternoon, however, activities had slowed, and when Marty came in, she felt as if she had just missed a party.

Douglas, the boy who helped out on Saturdays, was selling some tobacco to an old Negro man. The man ducked his wooly head, fumbling deep in the pockets of tattered overalls for his money. The laceless work boots on his feet were crusted over on the sides with dried red mud, and Marty could see a big dark toe at the end of the left shoe. The Negro never raised his eyes to the face of the white boy as he took the tobacco. "Yassuh, Mr. Douglas," he said, and shuffled out of the store.

Marty's uncle was coming out of the meat cooler, and he called out the familiar greeting he used each time the door whined open. "Somethin'?" Then he saw his niece. "Why, hey there, sugah. I didn't know that was you. This place has been workin' alive." His dark eyes beamed at her, partly with the excitement from the day's business, but mostly, she suspected, because he was glad to see her.

"I'm ready to help with those charge tickets you were talking about at dinner, Uncle Ray."

"We sure need 'em fixed up too. I separated 'em for you," he said, coming to stand beside Marty at the cash register. "This stack here is for the red box, and the rest for the green. All you got to do is put them behind the letter of their last name, like you did the other time."

Marty had helped with the tickets before and knew that the red file contained charges for tenant farmers, Negroes who worked land that was owned by her uncle. The reason for separating the tickets had never been revealed to her, but she knew it had something to do with Uncle Ray's bookkeeping system. Working for her uncle made Marty feel important, as if she were doing some grown-up job in a real office. Besides, she liked to see what people had bought.

Miss Julia had come in for two boxes of powdered pectin. Probably making some more jelly, thought Marty. Aunt Letta's friend Gertrude Parker must have had a headache this morning—one tin of Bayer. Ol' Tom, the Negro at the gas station, had potted meat and saltines for lunch. Ugh! Too bad he hadn't had some of Thelma's chicken.

"You got enough thread, Mary Claire?" Uncle Ray was speaking over his shoulder as he walked toward the cash register carrying a bolt of material.

"I got plenty, Ray, thank you, but you can put a card of these buttons on my ticket. See you got some good help here this afternoon. How you, Martha?"

Marty looked up from the tickets. "Just fine, Miz Cunningham. How's Little Earl doing?"

The long, dry face of the woman crinkled, and her cackle skipped about in the space overhead. "He's behavin' hisself, Martha, but I reckon we gon' have to start callin' him Big Earl directly. He's done growed up bigger than his daddy."

When the woman had gone, Uncle Ray went into the meat cooler at the rear of the store, and Marty returned to her work of sorting tickets. Sometime later she looked up to see her uncle standing beside her. "If you're nearly finished, you can ride out to Cole's with me to take him some feed."

Cole Reid was a tenant farmer who worked a piece of land belonging to Ray Armstrong at the edge of town. Although his son, Jun, was a few years older than Marty, she used to enjoy playing with him when she went with her uncle to take supplies to the Negro and his family.

"I've filed away all the tickets in the green box, but I have a few more for the red one. It'd be a whole lot easier, Uncle Ray, if we could put them all in one place anyway. Why do we have to keep them apart like this?"

She watched the face of her uncle darken, like somebody had pulled a shade down inside his head, taking the light away from his eyes. Now they looked like teddy bear eyes—flat, black, and cold. "Look here, hon," he said, scooping up the remaining tickets and laying them aside. "Don' be worryin' 'bout none of that business. Get yourself a Grapette to have on the way to Cole's, then go out to the truck. I'll be 'long directly."

Marty leaned back against the front left fender of the truck, her head tilted back, letting the cold sweet grapeness of the drink trickle down her throat. All at once something jabbed her ribs, and she jerked her head down, spewing the purple drink down her play-suit. A sound like rusty hinges came from behind her. She'd recognize that laugh anywhere, and she swung around, her eyes blazing.

"Jewel T. Turner, you're awful," she said, her hand brushing the front of her outfit. "Look what you made me do. Grapette all over myself."

Jewel was the son of Narvel Turner, who ran the seed store. He was a few years older than Marty, and she had always thought he was cute, despite the fact that he talked countrylike. She had told Anna Raye all about his dark curly hair and brown eyes that turned up at the corners. Marty wasn't quite sure why, but Jewel made her nervous. Maybe it was because of the stories she had heard from Thad about some of the trouble he'd been in.

"You sho' have changed since the last time I saw you, Martha Chafin," Jewel said, propping next to her on the fender. "How old are you now?" The dark eyes roamed from her hair to her feet and back again. Gosh, he made her feel funny.

"Not as old as you are, or as mean either." She wished Uncle Ray would hurry. "I'll smell like grape the rest of the day."

Jewel leaned over her chest, sniffing. "Oowee, smells sweet to me."

At that moment the screen door of the store clapped and Uncle Ray walked up. "Jewel, you go on now, and stop messin' with my girl."

"Yessir, Mr. Ray. I'll see you sometime, Martha." Jewel sidled off, grinning over his shoulder at Marty.

As her uncle pulled out onto the highway, Marty noticed the smoke from Sister's morning fires settling in the distance.

"Do you believe there's such a thing as witches, Uncle Ray?"

He gave a kind of grunt-chuckle. "I believe there's a bunch of mean women in this world. I sure believe that. Some right here in town too."

Was it possible her uncle knew about Ludie too? "Really? Who, Uncle Ray?"

"Well, Maybelle Turner didn't fix supper for a

week one time when Narvel bought hisself a shotgun instead of gettin' her new linoleum, and Gertrude locked Heywood Parker out of the house for two days 'cause he went fishin' and wouldn't carry her to see her people in Macon.''

"I don't mean normal kind of mean. I'm talkin' about scary mean." Marty leaned forward to watch her uncle's face. "Evil, like black magic and voodoo 'n all."

His eyes grew large and round, mockingly fearful, as he shrank back against the door of the truck. "Big black pots a-bubblin', and ugly ol' women putting spells on folks? That what you mean, sugah?"

"Yes! Things like that!" she cried, ignoring the ridicule in his eyes. "Witches with special powers to do bad things—witches who look horrible, like . . . like that Ludie person!"

Uncle Ray put his head back and roared. "Ludie?" He gasped between chuckles. "Ludie? A witch?"

Marty pushed on. "Okay. Laugh if you want to, but you just think about it. Sister with those pots of hers. How do you know they're not cooking something besides clothes back there?"

Suddenly her uncle's face was deadly serious. "You know, Martha, now that I think about it, you may be right. Lately, every time I put my head on one of those fresh-washed pillowcases Ludie brings back, I fall into a deep trance and don't wake up for hours and hours." He began to laugh again.

Marty sighed disgustedly and turned to face the window.

By this time they had reached the lane that led to Cole Reid's place, the tires of the truck straddling the weedy strip in the middle. Though it had never happened, Marty wondered what they would do if they met another vehicle, since there was room for only one and nothing on either side of the road but a deep ditch.

She propped her elbow on the open window of the truck, letting the warm air rush against her open palm. They were passing her uncle's fields now. A forest of corn grew straight and thick, and she could smell its raw greenness even through the dust of the road. Up ahead she saw the stand of plum trees, their branches overhanging the ditch at the side of the lane. They were getting close to Cole's.

Marty had made many such trips with her uncle out to the Negro tenant farmer's, swinging with his boy, Jun, in the old tire that hung by a rope from the chinaberry tree, or traipsing up the lane for plums while her uncle concluded his business with Cole.

Just as the face of her aunt and uncle's house seemed haughty and proud, so Cole's had an air of hollow sadness. Chickens and guinea hens scratched at the hard red earth around the house, which sat at the edge of a grove of trees. A chinaberry tree shaded the front edge of the house, and Marty noticed that the tire swing was gone. The dwelling itself was little more than a shack. Well, actually, it was a shack, thought Marty, and like most Negro houses, it was constructed of up-and-down unpainted boards, not side to side and painted like white people's.

Her uncle stopped the truck in the yard, scattering the hens. "Darlin', I believe you better stay here while I talk to Cole."

"I can't get out and see Jun?"

"He's not around today."

She watched through the rear window of the truck as her uncle and Cole hauled out the sacks of feed. As she turned around, she noticed a dark face disappearing at the back corner of the house. Jun, she thought, and immediately jumped out of the truck.

"Martha!" Her uncle's voice was severe as he dumped the feed on the porch and whirled to face her. "Get back in there. I'm comin' in a minute!"

Marty stood for an instant and considered disobeying her uncle, then slowly opened the door and climbed inside the pickup.

Cole and her uncle stood talking a few feet from the truck. The Negro stared at the ground, his frizzly head nodding from time to time at something Uncle Ray said. She couldn't hear much of the conversation—didn't care to, really. All she had wanted to do was go and say hello to Jun. What in the world was wrong with Uncle Ray today anyway? Acting so mean. First at the store when he looked so hateful at her about those silly tickets, and now not letting her go to see Jun when he knew perfectly well he was there.

"Boy hidey, Martha Chafin. Smells like grape perfume in here," he said, climbing into the truck beside her. "If I didn't know better, I'd think ol' Jewel was kinda taken with you 'while ago," he teased, reaching across and tousling her hair.

"Why couldn't I go see Jun?" she blurted out. She knew he was getting back to his normal self, teasing her about Jewel, but she wasn't ready. Not yet.

"Jun was busy, Martha. Helpin' his mama." Her uncle frowned slightly, pinching his lips together the way Miss Dozier did when she explained a math problem. "You know, honey, you're gettin' to be a young lady now. High time you put your childish ways behind you, like Paul says in Corinthians, 'bout puttin' away childish things."

"Jun's my friend. Friends aren't childish things."

She was certain she saw her uncle flinch. He cleared his throat, then spoke. "Let me see if I can say it right, Martha. What it boils down to is that some friends are just for childhood—then you outgrow 'em. Jun is somethin' like that . . . a playmate you had fun with when you were little. But now, well, you're growing up, and you oughtn' to be hangin' around with boys so much. People might get the wrong idea."

Marty moved to the edge of the seat so she could see his face as he drove. "But there aren't any girls my age down here."

"There's one or two, and your aunt Letta invited one of 'em home to dinner after church tomorrow. The little Harper girl, I believe, so y'all can—"

"You mean Janelle?" She was horrified. "She always smells like wet chickens. Also. . ." She paused before delivering what she considered the death blow to the subject of Janelle Harper. "Also, Daddy said y'all always thought of the Harpers as dirt-poor chicken farmers, and I'm not so sure he'd even want me socializing with her." Besides, she thought, I'm not going to let some chicken-smelling country girl mess up my plans to spy on Sister and Ludie.

"Martha Chafin!" You'd have thought she had said a bad word, her uncle sounded so shocked. His black eyebrows were pushed way up when he turned to look at her. "I'm surprised at you. Janelle is a nice girl, and her family has come up to some quality since George knew 'em. But the most important thing is being rich or poor ought not to matter. Underneath, everybody's the same. We all God's children, honey. Every last one of us. Don't ever forget that! And don't ever look down on folks 'cause they're different from you." He reached over and patted her leg. "Now I know you and Janelle gonna have a fine time."

By the time she drifted off to sleep that night, Marty had resigned herself to spending the boringest Sunday ever.

FOUR

Long ago Marty had decided that the best part about The Lord's Day in Caldwell, Georgia, was Thelma's Sunday dinner, which would be waiting when they got home. As soon as she realized Brother Mac wasn't going to say anything new, Marty donned her mask of thoughtful attention. Anyone seeing her would believe her to be completely mesmerized by the preacher: her head tilted slightly, an index finger nestled in the dimple of her cheek, and her eyes glued to the pulpit.

Actually her mind had more important things to do. First off it had to work out how to get rid of that chicken-drip Janelle Harper so she and Thad could investigate Sister and Ludie. If only she had a copy of *Modern Romance* from the box under her bed at home. One thing she knew—Aunt Letta's *Better Homes and Gardens* or *Collier's* wouldn't keep Janelle occupied very long. Maybe she could take her over to see Thad's postcards from all the places his mother had been; then they could sneak out on her, or maybe they could—

". . . and you know and I know, brothers and sisters, that if Jesus was to come to Caldwell this morning, His heart would break at seeing how we treat one another. Yessir!" Brother Mac slammed a bony fist on the pulpit, jarring Marty to attention. "Romans fourteen, verse ten: 'But why dost thou judge thy brother? Or why dost thou set at nought thy brother? For we shall all stand before the judgment seat of Christ!' That's right! All will be judged!"

How terrible! Uncle Ray had gone and told Brother Mac what she had said about Janelle. He must be preaching right at her.

"Our precious Savior's message is as plain as the nose on your face when he says 'Love' "—Brother Mac lengthened the word to two syllables so it came out "lu-uhv"—" 'your neighbor as yourself.' " The lanky preacher walked to the edge of the platform and looked directly at Marty. She held her breath. Suddenly he swung to the left and said quickly, "And that don't mean just the folks who live next door to you, now does it, Brother Cartwright?"

Marty exhaled. Thank goodness! He was after Mr. Cartwright.

The preacher pushed on. "No sirree! Your neighbor is each and every person in Caldwell. Each and every person in Georgia is your brother and your sister!" He paused, his hawklike eyes scanning the air above the congregation as if envisioning the entire universe gathered in that one room.

In spite of herself, Marty began mentally listing her "brothers and sisters." They passed in single file, smiling at her briefly before disappearing in her mind's mist: Mama, Daddy, Uncle Ray, Sara, Aunt Letta. Sara! Well, it was true, and she couldn't help it if Mama did have a "hissy" about it—she loved Sara like family! Why should you have to think about it anyway? Either you loved somebody or you didn't.

Mr. Cartwright was the only one who went down front at the invitational hymn to rededicate his life. Marty was certain he was in some kind of trouble. She wondered who Mr. Cartwright didn't love.

As soon as she saw Jewel Turner standing under tbe trees outside with his friends, Marty was glad she had worn her long-waisted dotted swiss. Aunt Letta was talking to Gertrude Parker, and Uncle Ray was still inside counting the collection. She decided to stroll casually across the yard and say hello to Miss Julia, thereby giving Jewel the benefit of her total appearance. But he was too busy talking to his buddies to give her a glance. They were laughing hard about something as she walked by. She said good morning to Miss Julia and stood with her and Mrs. Maybelle Turner near enough to the group of boys to be able to listen to their conversation. Her head turned sharply in their direction at the mention of Ludie.

"I guess he should have looked up ol' Ludie to get some of her potions." It was Little Earl Cunningham talking.

Marty felt her stomach shift. Potions! She knew she was a witch! She wished Mrs. Turner wouldn't talk so loud. She could hardly hear what the boys were saying.

"Them nigger fights is better than a pitcher show," she heard one of them say. "That's the good thing about summertime, going over yonder to the Red Goose Satidy night watchin' niggers cut one another up."

"If I was to bet, I wouldn't put much money on any of them field niggers, though," said Jewel. "They too tired workin' cotton to be much good. Too bad, too. I was hoping to see Jun Reid lay into that uppity Smith nigger. Last time he came in the store, he looked me smack in the eye, all smart-alecky."

"Yeah," put in Little Earl. "Ain't he the one that stayed up North? You got to watch them kind like a hawk."

"You know why come he went up there in the first place, don't you?"

"Naw."

"Yeah, he was the one argued with Mr. Ray Armstrong about cotton prices last year. His pa grows about twenty-five acres out toward Claxton for Mr. Ray, and at settlin' time, he claimed Mr. Ray was shortin' his daddy out of a hundred dollars. My pa said he eyeballed Mr. Ray with that know-it-all look that time, too, but Mr. Ray looked at him right back and said he best watch out how he disputes the word of a white man, else he liable to find hisself fanning the breeze from a tree some night."

When the laughter had died down, Marty heard Jewel speak again. " 'Course it don't matter to Mr. Ray anyway. He'd just get it back again, the way he fixes up his niggers' charge slips at the store." This brought another chuckle from the group.

"Hey, if you had to choose from bein' a hound dog or a nigger—"

"It don't make no difference. You can't get a lick of work out of either one, and you got to look after 'em both."

Martha Chafin hardly spoke on the ride back home, partly because she was thinking about the conversation she had overheard and partly because she didn't want that stringy-haired Janelle Harper to think she was going to be friendly.

Her "company," as Aunt Letta had called Janelle, sat silently, too, eyeing Marty shyly from under the large pink bow at the side of her head.

It doesn't help her looks, or that string hair, one

bit, Marty thought, bow or no bow. Her hair and eyes both are the color of dirty dishwater, and if she thinks I care about the junk she has in that paper sack, she's crazy. Marty turned her face to the window. If Uncle Ray did charge his tenant farmers more than other people, she was sure he had good reason. She knew her uncle Ray would never do anything dishonest, even to a colored. He was too good, for Christmas' sakes.

"You and Janelle go on in your room now, Martha, and change your Sunday clothes. Janelle, Martha will give you a hanger for your little dress so it don't get messed up, won't you, Martha?"

"Yes'm, Aunt Letta," Marty said. At least Janelle smelled like Evening in Paris today instead of chickens. "C'mon, Janelle," she said, making her voice sound bored.

After dinner the girls joined Marty's aunt and uncle on the porch, where they sat reading the Sunday paper. Marty had already decided to get up a game of Parcheesi with Uncle Ray, then set up a game between him and Janelle, giving her time to sneak over to Thad's. She set the game down on the porch floor. Her uncle peered over the top of the paper.

"Now, Martha. You know we don't play gambling games on Sunday, many times as you've been down here."

Her heart sank as she recalled the "shalt nots" for Sunday: no games with dice in them, no card games,

no sewing, no fishing, no buying, no this . . . no that
. . . almost no breathing.

"Why don't you and Janelle run over and sit in the
swing with Thad," said Aunt Letta. "After 'while you
can ride with Ray to take Thelma home."

The girls were almost to Miss Julia's when her
aunt's voice piped across the yard, shrill enough to
wake the dead. "Don't y'all talk too loud and wake up
Miss Julia from her Sunday nap, now, hear?"

"We won't."

"That's a real pretty sundress, Martha Chafin."
Janelle spoke hesitantly, as if she were afraid of addressing Marty.

"Uh-huh. Thank you, but it's called a pinafore.
Mama got it in Augusta," Marty replied tightly. What
a drip. Anybody should know the difference between
a pinafore and a sundress! Marty decided she had
better get some things straight. "Look, Janelle, Thad
and I had some plans for today. We were going to spy
on somebody who I think may very well be a real live
witch."

"Was you going to Sister and Ludie's house?"

Marty could not believe her ears. She stopped under
the magnolia tree and grabbed Janelle's wrist. "You
know about them?" she asked breathlessly.

"Well, my brother saw 'em in the yard one time.
He said they had some critters in some cages. And
Ludie was doing something to 'em."

"Was there a big black pot?"

"He didn't say. Jes' heard her whinin' at 'em."

"Probably putting a spell on them. Maybe turning them into something. Maybe draining out their blood. Maybe she's a vampire too." The words wouldn't come fast enough, as one idea after another tumbled about in Marty's head. "What else did your brother say?"

Janelle scratched her upper arm, rolling her eyes upward. "Ummmmm. He said it looked like she was makin' some potions. I b'lieve he did say he saw a big black pot. Said he saw Ludie give Sister somethin' to drink out'n it too."

"Hot diggity!" Marty clutched the girl's thin shoulders, then said patiently, "When we get to Thad's, you tell him everything you just said, you hear?"

"I will, Martha, I sho' will," said Janelle importantly.

When Janelle had finished, Marty got up from the steps and stood with one foot on the brick pillar. "Well? What have you got to say about that, Thad Walcott?"

"I'll believe it when I see it, that's all," answered Thad, working at a loose brick with his heel.

"You're gonna see it tomorrow. That's all there is to it," said Marty, sitting again beside Janelle on the steps. "Something else too. I heard Jewel and Little Earl Cunningham and some others talking at church about that fight at Red Goose last night. They said something about Jun being in it. Did he get hurt?"

"Nobody'd care if he did or didn't. Niggers fight like hound dogs. If you ask me, I'd be more worried about my dog being in a fight than any nigger, any day."

"Pa says his bird dog's got more sense than a dozen niggers," said Janelle, giggling.

"Well, I don't care what y'all say. Jun's different. He's always been a good friend of mine, and—"

"Martha, you can't have a nigger for a friend!" said Thad, looking over at Janelle. Marty watched their eyes meet briefly like they shared a secret. Then Janelle clamped her hands to her mouth to stifle a giggle.

"A nigger friend. Boy hidey," said Thad. He began to laugh, softly at first. Janelle joined in, and soon the two of them were rolling around on the steps like it was the funniest Abbott and Costello movie they had ever seen. Marty was sure Miss Julia's gray head would appear at the upstairs window any minute. It would serve them right, laughing so hard at her.

Marty felt her neck begin to get hot, and her heart raced. "You must not've been paying attention to what Brother Mac said this morning about not looking down on people," she told them angrily. "It's in the Bible."

"It don't mean about niggers." Thad's voice was muffled as he struggled to stop laughing.

"Niggers ain't but apes wearin' clothes. That's what my brother Quillan says," offered Janelle, producing another avalanche of tittering.

Marty rose and walked slowly down to the road,

staring at the deserted town in the distance. Sara, Thelma, Jun . . . apes? No! And why was it wrong to have a colored person for a friend? Strange new thoughts tumbled about in her head as she glanced across the field toward Sister's.

"Thad?" She turned back to the two on the porch. "Don't forget. We're going tomorrow right after breakfast. Janelle, we better go. It's time to take Thelma home."

FIVE

If there's not something good to see when we get there, you got to do everything I want to do, for the rest of your time in Caldwell."

"Thad," Marty wailed, "what do you mean? Didn't you hear one word Janelle said yesterday?" She took a leap to catch up to the boy ahead. "And don't walk so fast either. My legs aren't as long as yours."

They had crossed the state highway and just entered the weedy field that led to the woods in front of Sister's place. Thad carried his Red Ryder BB gun, "in case we run into any snakes," and Marty had a sack of sandwiches and a jar of water.

She had kind of told Aunt Letta a story about her plans for the morning.

"A clubhouse? In the woods? With Thad?" Aunt Letta's face had screwed up like she smelled something awful. "Martha Chafin, when you gonna grow up and quit all them tomboy things anyway? You ought to stay and see how Thelma and me make preserves."

If I didn't have anything better to do than watch somebody cook something, I guess I'd go on and die right now, Marty had thought.

She and Thad were deep into the field, pushing the leggy wildflowers and rabbit tobacco aside with their knees.

"Just remember, though, Thad. We didn't actually make a pact or anything about that business of doing what you want to. That was all your idea. All I said was, 'Uh-huh, maybe.' Besides, your idea of seeing something good and mine may not be the same." Marty put the jar of ice water against her hot face, pausing to look back at the houses in the distance.

"There's heaps better things to do than go watch some ol' nigger woman, 's all I know." Thad swung his gun to his shoulder and nodded toward the trees ahead. "C'mon, let's hurry and get in the woods. It'll be cooler in there," he said, and broke into a trot.

Marty was right behind him, and within seconds they stood panting amid massive columns of pine bark that stretched out of sight to green-needled branches swaying overhead.

"It smells funny in here, like medicine." Marty kicked up the carpet of pine needles.

"Ain't you ever smelled pine tar before?" The boy walked on a bit before stopping at the base of a tree and sitting down. "Let's have some water, but be careful you don't lean up against that tree. You'll get tar on your shirt."

Marty sat Indian fashion, across from Thad, on a soft cushion of brown straw and poured water into two cups. "It's still cold," she said, handing him a cup. "Do you want your sandwich now too?"

"I reckon so. Else I'll probably be too scared in a minute to eat it." His voice took on a false whimper and his green eyes looked mockingly at Marty.

She knew he was making fun of her. "I just hope you get scared half out of your wits, Thad Walcott. I swanee, the facts are plain as the nose on your face, plus what Janelle said her brother saw." Marty opened her sandwich and wiped off some of the mayonnaise with her napkin. She was silent, staring thoughtfully at the open sandwich in her hand.

"What's the matter?" he asked. "A bug get on your baloney?"

"Uh-uh. I was thinking about something."

"What?"

"Oh, about maybe that we're getting too big to do things like this—adventures 'n all."

"Maybe," replied Thad, taking a bite from his sandwich. "Seems like girls grow up sooner than boys."

He paused, and Marty glanced up to see him staring hard at her.

Oh Lordy, I hope he's not gonna get embarrassing!

"But"—Thad continued to look at her—"just because they grow up faster don't make 'em any smarter." He swatted at a big, blue-green horsefly buzzing about his head. "Talkin' the way you did in front of Janelle Harper was plain out stupid."

"About Sister and Ludie?"

"No!" He sounded almost angry. "About Jun Reid being some kind of friend of yours. Just don't talk about things like that down here, Martha. Not ever!" He had been folding up the waxed paper from his sandwich as he spoke, and now he flung it behind him and rose, brushing his hands on his shorts.

She wanted to ask him what he meant by what he had just said, but by the time she got to her feet, he was off again and she had to run hard to catch up.

They did not go far before the air grew warm and the smell of the hickory fire became strong. Marty knew they would be coming out of the woods soon. Her heart beat faster as she thought of what lay ahead. Thad continued to lead the way, his steps slowing deliberately as they neared light. Suddenly he stopped, putting an arm out behind him. "Shhh. We're close enough. Get behind that tree."

Thad had chosen a pair of large pines with a good viewpoint. From her tree Marty could see not only the front of Sister's house, but one whole side and a part of the backyard as well. Her eyes widened as she studied the house.

She had expected it to look like Cole Reid's, or any other Negro cabin. Instead of the usual unpainted vertical boards, though, Sister's house was built of concrete blocks, painted white. Brick pillars supported a long front porch, and the steps leading up to it were concrete, not rickety wooden, like Cole's. Other than a few patches of rust on the tin roof, the house didn't look bad at all to Marty. The dirt in the front yard had recently been swept with a yard broom, and on either side of the steps a whitewashed tire held a bed of purple petunias.

"It looks nicer than I thought," she whispered across to Thad.

"Don't it look witchy enough to suit you?"

A whimper from the back of the house drew their attention to that area. Beneath a low-hanging chinaberry tree were four crates with wire fronts. The sound had come from one of them.

"Thad, look!" Marty said urgently. "Those cages in back, under the tree. Animals are in 'em, see? A squirrel, and a raccoon or something."

"I guess. Looks like it anyway."

"I think I see one of the pots too. See that black thing? Gosh a'mighty, I wish I could see better. I wonder—" The snap of a screen door from the back silenced Marty, and she flattened herself against a tree.

Cautiously she edged around the tree. "It's her. It's Ludie!" Marty stared, her scalp tingling, as the Negro hobbled toward one of the cages, making gurgling noises. Marty thought she was even more gruesome than she remembered, as she watched Ludie thrust a twisted arm inside a cage and take out the raccoon. She held the animal high over her head with her good arm, and Marty was glad her back was turned to them as a fiendish cry clawed the air. Suddenly Marty's stomach churned. Ludie was approaching the spot where the pot seemed to be, the furry raccoon still aloft. Oh, if only she could see more! Or did she even want to?

Thad spoke slowly, his voice quivering. "It's goin' in the pot . . . she's gon' drown him!" He turned to Marty, his eyes even larger than normal.

"I told you!" Her voice was teary. "I can't stand to watch!"

"Let's go! 'Fore she sees us!" said Thad, backing away for a few steps before turning and breaking into a run.

Marty caught up with him in the middle of the woods, but the two did not stop running until they came out into the blazing sun on the other side.

"What'd I tell you? If that's not a witch, I don't know what is." They walked more slowly now, and Marty cut her eyes shyly to the boy beside her. "Too bad you were such a fraidycat. I wanted to see Sister too."

"Me?" His voice squeaked. "You're the one said you couldn't stand to watch! You want to go back, Miss Brave Mary Marvel?"

"I can't. Aunt Letta wants me to ride into Claxton after dinner."

"Well, just remember. It wasn't me got scared. I didn't see nothing bad enough to get scared about."

Marty was glad she had to go to Claxton.

SIX

An outing to Claxton, Georgia, was a special occasion to most everybody in Caldwell, since it was the closest thing to a city for miles around. Claxton had industry (the Graco Mills), politics (county seat of Gray County), transportation (Southern Railway and a Trailways depot), and commerce (mainly Phelps Department Store, where Aunt Letta sometimes bought ready-made clothes). Since she lived in a city at least three times the size of Claxton, Marty was not impressed with the town, although she had to admit it was better than spending the afternoon "rocking to China" or listening to Aunt Letta's Bing Crosby records.

During the twelve-mile ride from Caldwell Aunt Letta had chirped away, first repeating the lecture Uncle Ray had given to Marty on Saturday about "going off in the woods with boys," and then, without taking a good breath, reciting her shopping plan for the day and what she intended to do with the things she bought when she got home. Marty had not paid attention to the shopping list, because she was still trying to sort out the reason for the sudden interest in her own activities.

"Thank the good Lord. There's a parking space right across from Phelps." Aunt Letta wheeled the car into position in front of the Gray County Courthouse on Claxton's town square.

The square was a parklike area with tree-shaded walks and gray wooden benches. The courthouse stood in the center, stories higher than the other buildings in town, its Georgian front facing them with patrician aloofness. Stores and offices rimmed the streets opposite the square, and as she got out of the car, Marty noticed that *Tarzan's Savage Fury* was playing at the Capitol Theater.

Marty would have preferred coming to Claxton on a Friday or Saturday, when the movie would be open, but her aunt said it would be "workin' alive with nigrahs."

Aunt Letta took a handkerchief from her purse and

waved at the air in front of her face. "Gosh sakes. Must be a hundred and ten here. Glad it's not this way back home."

"I believe it would be a good day to go to Walgreen's for a Coke float, don't you, Aunt Letta?" Marty knew that the drugstore was always the last stop for an afternoon in Claxton.

"You know your aunt Letta's gon' wind up at Walgreen's when we come to Claxton, don't you, sugah?" Her aunt laughed shrilly, causing a Negro woman standing outside Phelps to peek out from under her parasol and grin.

Phelps was nothing like the shiny, air-conditioned stores in Augusta. Large, noisy fans on tall stands and an occasional overhead fan did little more than stir the air, which was only slightly cooler than outside. Wooden floors creaked under shoppers' feet, and merchandise was displayed on heavy wooden counters and tables. Marty stopped at the jewelry counter, fingering a chalk-white choker.

"I'm gon' up and get my bedspread out of layaway," Aunt Letta told her. She was doing over a room to match one she had seen in *Better Homes and Gardens.* "When I come down, you can take it to the car and I'll meet you at the hardware store."

Marty watched her aunt disappear behind the brass cage of the elevator before turning back to the jewelry counter. A child's wail twisted her head sharply in the direction of the water fountain.

At the "White Only" fountain a Negro woman was holding a small boy by one elbow, shaking him roughly. "I tol' you, dis yo' watuh ovuh heah, boy. Why you haffa gimme sech a time, wif you hans all ovuh white folks' spigot? You gon' git us run out'n dis sto. Come on ovuh heah wheah you b'long to be." She pulled the boy a few feet away, to the fountain marked "Colored."

Marty leaned against the counter, observing the scene. While his mother took a drink from the fountain, the boy clung to her skirts, looking up at Marty. His dark eyes were still moist, and as they looked first at her and then over to the "white" fountain, the question she saw in them was as plain as the color of his face.

Once when she had been about the age of the child in front of her, she had made a similar error, running to the wrong fountain in a large Augusta store. She could still feel Mama's hand firmly on her small shoulders, marching her over to the "right" place. Later, when she had asked her mother, Beth Armstrong had explained that she would get germs if she drank after coloreds.

Marty had not thought of the incident for many years, but the bewilderment on the face of the small boy sent time rushing backward. She had been puzzled, too, but had not known enough to question further. After all, when you're four years old, you believe that the wisdom of the world is in the heads of your mama and daddy, and if they say coloreds have germs, then surely the poor things must be working alive with them. She continued to stare at the "colored" sign over the fountain long after the woman had taken the child away.

"Martha, Martha Chafin, honey . . . you 'sleep?" Aunt Letta was at her side.

"Oh, I'm sorry, Aunt Letta. Guess I was day-dreaming."

Her aunt thrust a fluffy brown package at her. "Go on and put this in the trunk of the car, if you will. Here's the keys now. I'm gon' look at drapes, then I'll be over at Johnson's directly."

When she had deposited the package in the trunk of the car, Marty hooked the keys around her index finger, then started back across toward Johnson's Hardware Store. The day was white hot, and the heat from the pavement pushed up hard, stinging her face. She was glad to get under the awning of the hardware store, away from the scorching sun. Presently she heard voices coming from the stairway that led to the dentist's office over Johnson's.

A young, coffee-colored Negro woman clumped down the wooden stairs and stood in the doorway. Sunlight danced in the black ringlets of her hair, and Marty could see that although her face was wrenched in pain, she was very pretty. The young woman pressed a cloth against one side of her face, and her words were slurred as she looked up the stairs and spoke.

"Den'is' Jack, I ain't able to git to A'gusta today to see no coluhd den'is'. If yo' jes' lemme come on back affah dark lak—"

Heavy steps thundered down the stairway and a white man appeared, wearing the white smock of a dentist. He took the girl by the arm and forced her against the wall. Marty moved away, embarrassed to let them see her, but she continued to listen.

"Mattie!" The man spoke sharply. "In the first place I told you never, ever to come here during the day. And in the second place, I do not—do not, do you understand—treat nigrahs, ever! I don't care who they are! Now, take this money and get yourself on over to Augusta like I told you. I'll talk to you later."

He shoved the woman out to the sidewalk, and she stumbled off, sniffling and shaking her head from side to side.

Marty's eyes followed the Negro down the street; then she turned her head to look again at the empty stairwell. "For Christmas' sakes," she said softly. "He didn't have to act so ugly."

For the second time that day Marty's young frame sagged beneath the weight of unexplainable sadness. I've been around colored people all my life, she thought. And I never realized how different things are for them . . . ordinary, everyday things. She passed a hand over her forehead to clear her mind of these new ideas that wanted to crowd in. "Shoot," she told herself. "I'm just having growing pains. That's all." Then, with a toss of her head she shook off the burden of the two incidents and skipped down the sidewalk to the drugstore.

But while waiting for her aunt outside Walgreen's, Marty was bothered once more by the memory of the inquiring eyes of the child in Phelps and the anguish in those of the woman who had rushed past her. Presently she became aware of a new idea shaping itself in her mind. Questions and pain. The two words loomed large before her like signposts at a crossroads. Perhaps if she had had the answers to her questions when she was younger, the pain would have been too great. Her head nodded slowly, agreeing with itself.

Later at Walgreen's, one of the few air-conditioned businesses in Claxton, Marty leaned back in her chair and lifted dank strands of hair from her neck. She was savoring the delicious coolness of the store nearly as much as the Coke float she had just finished.

Aunt Letta *slurggled* the last bit of ice cream through her straw, then wiped her mouth. She reached beneath her chair and brought out a Phelps bag. "Bought you a pretty, 'while ago," she said to Marty, pulling a white straw pocketbook from the sack.

"Oh, Aunt Letta. I love it. It'll go good with my white shoes for church."

"That's what I thought too." Her aunt's face was washed with a soft glow, and Marty decided that if there was anything unjust going on in the world, the dear soul behind those warm gray eyes had nothing to do with it.

Marty was in high spirits as she left the drugstore with Aunt Letta. She held her head high and hummed "My Cup Is Full and Running Over" softly as she rounded the corner by Walgreen's. A shadow clouded her sunny mood for an instant when she saw the little colored boy from Phelps standing at the "Colored Service" window on the sidewalk outside Walgreen's, but she kept humming. After all, it wasn't her fault everybody wasn't born white.

SEVEN

The butter puddle broke over the wall of grits and ran in rivulets toward the two eggs on Marty's plate. She eyed the crawl of the yellow stream, nibbling absently on a link of sausage in her fingers.

"Yo' breakfas' gon' git colt, don' you goan 'n eat." Thelma observed Marty's plate from her place at the sink.

Marty went to the back door, craning her neck for signs of her aunt. She came back and took her plate to the sink. "Listen, Thelma. You know I can't eat this much food first thing in the morning. I'm just not used to it." She tilted her face toward Thelma's and smiled sweetly. "Remember how you used to eat my leftover breakfast? Remember you always cleaned up my grits for me?"

"I 'membuhs how I used to fin' rings o' grits squonched up 'neath yo' plate, wheah you done squonched 'em so Miss Letta b'lieve you et 'em. I 'membuhs dat." Thelma was taking a hard line this morning.

"Please, Thelma?" Marty set the plate at the woman's elbow. "I go 'round with my stomach about to pop open the whole time I'm in Caldwell, from eating so much."

"It be poppin' from all dem sweets you be eatin' out'n Mistah Ray's sto', is why it be poppin'. Yo' auntie done tol' you dey don' do nothin' 'cept make holes in yo' teeth."

Marty had started to leave the kitchen, but stopped in the doorway, turning back to Thelma.

"Thelma. You ever have a toothache?"

"Don' eat gracious lots o' sweets."

"No, but did you ever, when you were little, maybe, have to go to the dentist for anything?"

"Ain't no coluhd den'is'." The dark eyes were puzzled.

"I was just wondering, that's all, about what y'all . . . about what colored people did about toothaches and cavities and all."

Thelma turned back to her kitchen chores, frowning. "Seems lak I r'cleck Auntie Eastuh's smallest granbaby come down wid a so' tooth some time back. Carried dat chile off someplace far to see to huh tooth."

"To Augusta?"

"Dat soun' right."

Marty exhaled loudly and walked slowly out to the back porch, sitting on the steps. She could see Aunt Letta's straw hat bobbing to and fro as she worked at the flowers in her garden. For an instant Marty considered going to help her. No. She couldn't be that desperate for something to do. Miss Julia had taken Thad into Claxton to see the eye doctor—not that he was all that much fun anymore. Oh well, she could always drag out Nancy Drew.

A squirrel scampered down the big oak tree at the corner of the house, stopped short at her feet, then whirled and bounded back up the trunk of the tree. "You don't have to be scared of me, little thing," she called after him. "I'm not going to put you in a pot and boil you up." A light switched on in her head, and Marty snapped her fingers. She had just decided how to spend the morning.

Her face was flushed and her heart pounded as Marty raced down the lane to the state highway. She felt bad about not telling anyone where she was going, but shoot, she was almost thirteen. Why should she have to report every little move?

At the highway she paused to let a truck pass, and nearly turned back when she recognized the truck belonging to Jewel Turner's daddy, Narvel. Quickly she began pulling black-eyed Susans at the side of the road to make it appear she was just gathering flowers. When the truck had rounded the curve into town, Marty dashed across the highway, her sandals flapping against the hot gravel. She stopped at the edge of the field, remembering that she hadn't worn her oxfords. Then, deciding she couldn't risk going back, she plunged into the high, dry weeds. Her feet barely touched the ground as she leaped and scrambled through the tall brush, not stopping until she had safely reached the first line of trees in the woods. There she rested shortly before entering the forest.

"There's nothing to be afraid of in here," she told herself reassuringly. Really, it was kind of nice being there alone. Dim and quiet, like an Episcopal church she had gone to one time with Anna Raye.

Marty passed the spot where she and Thad had rested, making a note to pick up the jar and sack they had left from the day before. Today was going to be a lot different!

As the clearing came into view, Marty's steps slowed. She looked around, searching for a vantage point from which she could see the entire backyard. To the right of the house was a vegetable garden, which offered no place to hide. At the left, the tall pines of the woods thinned to a sparse stand of hardwoods, but these stood in tangled undergrowth, impossible to reach. She had no choice but to return to the same area as yesterday.

The bark on the pine tree was rough against her face and the tar of the tree stung her nose slightly as she looked out from the woods. Sister's house seemed the same; the yard was brushed, petunias nodded in their tire beds, crates at back under the chinaberry tree. Her eyes strained to see into the backyard, and she discovered that by lying flat she could see underneath the house, straight through from front to back. Between the brick pillar and the front steps there was a clear view of the cages and the backyard.

A short distance beyond the cages were several more whitewashed tires with plants growing in them. Marty watched, unmoving, until she saw the dark feet and familiar blue skirt come into view. She sat up quickly. She simply had to see what was going on back there. Could she get to the side of the house? Slowly she edged up the trunk of the tree, keeping watch. She was sure she could make the distance between the woods and the house without being seen, and after scanning the area once more, dashed toward the house, ducking down at the porch.

Raising herself slowly, Marty pressed back against the cool concrete wall of the cabin, then moved toward the rear, her legs crisscrossing its length from front to back. She swallowed hard before placing her right cheek against the side of the house, then carefully allowed her left eye a clear view of the rear yard.

Ludie was there all right. A knife in her hand sent a shiver up Marty's spine, but she resolved to keep her eyes on the scene in the yard. To her relief, she saw Ludie use the knife to snip some of the plants growing in the tires. The Negro moved to another tire, collected more clippings, and put them into a dented bucket on the ground. Marty was so engrossed, she never heard the footsteps behind her.

"You be wantin' Ludie, Miss?"

With a muffled yelp Marty threw herself against the house.

A tall Negro boy stood before her, nestling a small squirrel against his chest with his right arm. A sling of printed material held his left. The frazzled edge of his overalls hung nearly a foot above his bare feet, and his face was all grin, causing his cheekbones to protrude like two shiny brown knobs.

"You after Ludie, Miss?" he repeated.

Marty pushed her voice past the rock-hard lump in her throat. "Not especially. Uh . . . I wanted . . ." Marbles rolled around in her brain. "Do you, um, live here?"

He cast his eyes down, shifting the animal in his arms. "Be Chili, Ludie's bro. This my mama's place."

Marty thought frantically. How could she explain herself? Why hadn't she stayed and helped Aunt Letta?

Steps were heard across the back porch, and Marty looked up to see a meaty Negro woman with pigtailed hair bending over the edge of the porch. "Chili? Who speakin'?"

Marty saw the woman's dark face widen in surprise and two pudgy hands come together under her chin. "Bless mah soul! Mistah Georgie's chile. I know you anytime—you the pitchuh o' yo' daddy!"

Marty nodded dumbly and moved to the steps at the back of the porch, her eyes on Ludie.

The woman waddled down the steps and turned to the boy. "Miss Martha, Chili. Mistah Georgie's." She stood in front of Marty, shaking her head from side to side, hands on her hips. The next instant the thick lips parted and Sister's throaty laugh echoed in the yard.

"Bet you don' 'membuh ol' Sistah mindin' you when yo' was a tiny thing, jes' holdin' yo' het up, does you?"

"I don't think so." Marty was becoming calmer. The person before her seemed harmless enough; like any other old Negro woman.

"Well, chile." Sister's eyes glowed with friendship. "You sho' nuff have growed. Lemme see. Miss Letta send you fo' somethin'?" She turned toward Ludie, who had been standing, watching from her place beside the cages. "Ludie? You carry Miss Letta huh jelly?"

The warped face moved up and down rapidly.

"Uh, Sister." Marty swallowed. "Aunt Letta didn't send me. I went for a walk in the woods, and well . . ." She forced her mouth into a smile. "Before you know it, here I was."

"Well, we glad you drap in, Miss Martha." Sister looked at her son. "Chili, yo' sistah waitin' fo' dat animal too." As she turned to go up the steps of the porch, the woman said to Marty, "Miss, you maybe lak to watch how Ludie do. She sometime half magic wid dem animals o' huhs."

As she approached the young Negro woman, Marty forced herself to explore her face. If you tried, you could make out the shape of Africa from the appliqué of brown skin over her cheek. It wasn't too scary if you looked at it with that in mind. It was just Africa, for Christmas' sakes. The skin was creased around Ludie's eyes, but they beamed like lanterns, and the left side of her face turned up sharply. *I guess she calls herself smiling,* Marty decided.

Chili transferred the baby squirrel into Ludie's outstretched hand. "Ludie lak doin' huh animals."

Marty's stomach yo-yoed as she remembered the scene she and Thad had witnessed. "What . . . what does she . . . she do to them?" she stammered.

Ludie sat beside the bucket, cradling the squirrel and crooning. Though her voice rose and fell in the same rhythmic strains, it was softer, less frightening, than the eerie song Marty recalled from that first morning.

Chili hunched down next to his sister. "She do fo' 'em when dey hurts, or when dey mama gits kilt o' go off and leave 'em. Always sing to 'em fo' she start in, lak dis. Make 'em still, fo' dey treatmint."

Marty eased herself down to sit on the edge of one of the tire gardens. "What's wrong with him?" she asked, her eyes on the squirrel.

"Mos' likely he mama gots kilt. She fin' him 'neath a tree day fo' yestiddy, all puny. Den tak'n some o' dem yarbs she keeps stirred up 'n give him. Now he holt up his het real good. Sometime dey jes' need to be cleaned up from de ticks 'n lice 'n sech, and she give 'em a good dippin' in de pots and dey gits bettuh."

Dipping in the pot? Marty spied the black pot that had caused her so much anxiety. So that's what Ludie had been doing yesterday!

The squirrel lay motionless on his back in Ludie's lap as her gnarled fingers stroked his stomach soothingly. Presently Marty saw her reach into the bucket and withdraw a jar containing an amber-colored liquid. Ludie gave it to Chili, who opened it and set it on the ground. From the folds of the blue skirt an eyedropper appeared, and after filling it from the jar, Ludie pushed the tiny tube between the animal's teeth. Some of the liquid ran down his whiskers, and Marty watched, fascinated, while the feeding was repeated.

"What's in the jar?" she asked Chili.

"Ludie?" he said, turning to his sister.

"Yaanh," she replied, nodding toward one of the tires.

"Be yellowroot leaves, brewed up. Be good fo' buildin' blood. She use cherry bark drippin's some, too, but ain't time o' year fo' dem."

Chili got to his feet and Marty followed.

"Do you always help her like this?"

Ludie pointed to the sling on her brother's arm. "Na naanh . . ." Her mouth moved strangely, as if she were trying to say something more; then she shrugged and shook her head hopelessly.

"Dem's all Ludie's doin's," Chili replied, gesturing at the cages. He touched the sling on his arm. "I jes' be home now since I hurt mah arm and cain't go in de fields fo' a bit."

Ludie got to her feet and nudged Marty's arm gently with the tiny animal. Marty's face was inches from the older girl as she took the squirrel. Really, she thought, Thad's right. She's just a Negro that got burned up.

Marty petted the squirrel as she walked around the yard. It seemed likely that Ludie possessed some sort of magic powers, for Marty had never known a squirrel so tame. She guessed it had been dumb of her to come here, but she was still glad she had seen for herself. It was like being afraid to take a test, then finding out you knew most of the answers. Overcoming fear made you feel grown up. Not that there was anything to be afraid of here, she thought, remembering Ludie's gentleness with the animal and the look of pride in Chili's eyes as he watched his sister.

"Waanh . . ." Ludie jerked her head toward the last cage.

"She say it b'long in de cage now." Chili bent and unlatched the door of the crate at the end of the row.

Marty deposited the animal, then straightened. She looked at Ludie, then at Chili. "Chili, how do you know what Ludie's saying?" She kept her voice low.

"You be 'roun' some, you know." The boy threw his shoulders back and lifted his chin slightly. "Ludie got sense. She jes' cain't speak, 's all."

The sun was high in the sky now, and Marty knew she should start back, but she was reluctant to leave. She liked the quiet, simple world of Ludie and Chili and wanted to know more. "Do you think it would be okay if I came back tomorrow and, maybe, helped Ludie with her animals, or something?" she asked Chili.

They had walked around to the side of the house, and Chili looked at the woods beyond, as if he could see her uncle's house right through them. He shook his head, frowning. "Ah cain't say. Mayn't be right. Reckon yo' auntie say so, it'd be all right."

A bubble of discontent rose for a second inside Marty, then broke as she pushed it down. She wasn't exactly sure why, but she made up her mind right then that for a time, anyway, she would keep her association with Sister and her family a secret.

On her way back through the woods she picked up the jar and sack. These would explain her absence of this morning if necessary.

By the time she passed beneath the two pecan trees in the front yard, her mind had tucked away several alibis for other days.

As she mounted the steps to the front porch, she met a wall of dinner smells. Overcoming fear made you feel grown up, but it also made you very, very hungry.

Uncle Ray leaned back from the table, patting his paunch with both palms. "Thelma," he called, leaning sideways toward the kitchen door, "I'm ready for banana puddin' anytime." He rested his arms on the table and turned to his wife. "Speakin' of puddin', Letta, somebody came in the store this morning asking after our little ol' puddin' head." He winked and nodded in Marty's direction.

"Asking after me?" She cocked her head and wrinkled her nose at her uncle.

"You the only puddin' head I know of in this house."

"Who was it, Uncle Ray? Who was asking?"

Her uncle swallowed a spoonful of dessert, then took a long drink of iced tea, his dark eyes dancing at her over the rim of his glass.

"Come on, Uncle Ray. Who?"

"Now who did I tell you the other day I thought was gettin' sweet on you?"

"Sweet on Martha?" Aunt Letta sounded astonished. "Why, she's too young for all that business, Ray. Who was it anyway?"

"Martha Chafin knows. And in case you hadn't noticed, Letta, our little gal is nearly gone. We just about got ourselves a young lady."

"Jewel! That's who it was, waddn't it, Uncle Ray? What'd he say about me?" Martha felt giddy, stifling a giggle. Jewel, my gosh.

"Ohh, he wanted to know what you been up to since you been here. Said he might walk over if he goes to see Thad someday soon." Her uncle wiped his mouth and got up from the table.

Marty concentrated on her pudding, feeling her face grow rosy. She didn't dare look up and let them see how Jewel's attentions had affected her.

"Why, Jewel don't run around with Thad, Ray," Aunt Letta said.

"I know he don't, Letta," Uncle Ray spoke patiently to his wife. "That's what gave it all away." He turned to Marty as he started from the room. "How'd you like to ride back to the store and keep me company this afternoon, sugah?"

She thought for a minute of refusing, then decided it might give her an opportunity to bring up the subject of Ludie and her visit with the family across the high-way. That is, if it came just right. "Okay, let me brush my hair first and change my blouse."

From her room, minutes later, she could hear her aunt talking to her uncle.

"See what all yo' talk about Jewel's done? Now you got that child wantin' to fix herself up fo' the boys. I declare, Ray, first thing you know, we'll be beatin' 'em off with a stick when she comes down here."

Marty giggled out loud, picturing her uncle standing on the porch swatting at a crowd of young boys.

EIGHT

The following morning pushed itself boldly through the chintz curtains of Marty's bedroom. She sensed its brightness but did not open her eyes, and had it not been for two bobwhites in some distant part, vying for the last word, she would have buried her head and made the day wait.

She rolled, stretching and yawning, onto her stomach, her nose filling with the hair smells from the pillow. As her mind began to clear, she was aware of a nagging darkness within her. Worry pawed at her like her cat, Whipper, with a June bug—swatting and pushing before finally falling upon it. What had happened to make her feel so bad? She flopped over onto her back and tried to remember. Yes, now she knew. She had dreamed, and the dream was making her sad, lingering in her mind like the aftertaste of awful medicine.

She had been somewhere with Mama and Daddy, some place with animals, such as a farm. A zoo! It had been a zoo, kind of. The place began to take shape again in her mind. There had been rooms, but she had been unable to see anything inside, just shadows. Then they had walked down a long hall to a place outside, a place with trees all around. There had been a huge building with bars on one side. No, it wasn't a building. It was a cage! A big cage, much like the ones in which Ludie kept her animals, only big, so much bigger than Ludie's, and there had been a tree growing right inside it. Sitting and hanging about the tree, like monkeys, were dozens of Negroes, different shades of brown and beige; men, women, children. She had recognized Sara, Thelma, the young woman from the dentist's office. Ludie, too, or someone wearing her blue skirt, except this girl's body wasn't twisted. Her daddy had laughed. Mama was smiling too.

Marty sat up, hugging her knees to her chest, against the headboard. That was all she could remember, all her mind would sketch.

She got up and stood beside the bed, then began to remove her nightgown. Quickly, almost fiercely, she pulled it over her head, as if by getting rid of it she could somehow shed her somber mood. In the bathroom she splashed water over her face and looked into the mirror. Drops of water slid down her cheeks and clung to her chin. The electric-blue eyes stared at her. "What in the world's gettin' into you?" she asked the auburn-haired girl in the mirror. "It was only a dream, for gosh sakes." She brushed her teeth and slipped the brush into its holder. Just the same, she couldn't wait to get to Ludie's.

"Well, good mornin', merry sunshine." When Aunt Letta was present, the kitchen in the morning reminded Marty of a film she had seen in social studies showing the factories and sweatshops during the Industrial Revolution. Not at all like the quiet morning kitchen of her mother. " 'Fraid you're gonna have to grab a doughnut and call it good this morning, Martha," said her aunt. "I've got Thelma busy helpin' me put my dish together for my circle meetin'."

Good news, thought Marty, thankful to escape the usual hefty breakfast. "What time are you going?" she asked, eager to start for Ludie's.

"In a minute. I should be back right after y'all have your dinner."

Marty took a doughnut and a glass of milk to the front porch and sat in a rocker. There was no breeze this morning, and the air was thick against her skin. Even the sweetness of the honeysuckle weighed so heavy, it seemed to take shape around her. From Miss

Julia's vine-covered porch came the song of the swing, and she knew Thad was there. Shoot, now she not only had to shed Aunt Letta but Thad, too, before starting for Sister's. Oh, Lord, maybe he was there for the duration. She'd better find out.

Brushing the doughnut's powdered sugar from her shorts and setting the empty glass aside, she walked to the side of the porch. "Thad, you get your glasses yesterday?"

The creak stopped and the chains shifted as Thad turned to talk to her. She knew he could see her through the vines, but she couldn't see him. "Uh-uh. I got to go back Friday morning."

"What are you going to do this morning?" Marty asked, hoping he wouldn't interfere with her plans.

"Got to help Bigmama get ready for Mother coming on Saturday." For some reason Thad had always referred to his parents as Mother and Father. Probably the influence of his Yankee daddy.

"Are you glad your mama's coming?"

"I'll be real glad to see her, but then she's gonna carry me back yonder with her for the summer."

"To New York City? Gosh. Lucky dog." Marty jumped down off the porch and crossed the yard, peering through the vines at Thad's face.

"She don't live there now. They live in Chicago." Marty heard him sigh. "I wish they'd just move to Georgia. I don't really want to go up North."

"I think it'd be fun. Besides, you'll see some movie

stars, probably, or somebody else famous." Marty had always believed that the mysterious metropolises of the North were the nesting places of all celebrated people.

"Trouble is," Thad drawled, "they got too many Yankees up there. Every time I have to go, I'm scared of gettin' a little more Northernized or somethin'."

"Your daddy's a full-fledged Yankee, so that makes you half one already."

"No, he iddn't. He's from Baltimore, Maryland," Thad said indignantly. "Besides, even if it is up there, Maryland liked the South better in the War between the States. I just—"

"Thayad . . . come on in now," Miss Julia cawed from upstairs.

Thad continued, ignoring his grandmother, "I just got through readin' about it."

"Huh. He still talks like one, 's all I know," said Marty, moving off. "Guess I'll see you tomorrow."

As Marty climbed the porch steps, she heard her aunt's car start up in the back, and she waved good-bye as the car backed out of the driveway. At last she could claim the day.

Ludie was sitting on the front steps when Marty came out of the woods. A thick book lay in her lap, and beside her a pad and pencil. When she noticed Marty, she waved. The young Negro seemed different somehow, and for an instant Marty wondered if she had straightened Ludie's body with her dream. Then as she drew nearer she realized Ludie had only changed clothes. She wore a soft red-and-white gingham skirt and a clean white blouse, and even though she had changed the scarf over her head, it was still blue. Must be blue's one of her favorite colors, thought Marty. At least she's not in a cage, even if her body is still messed up. She sat next to her new friend, leaning over Ludie's lap to get a better look at the catalog that lay there.

Ludie pointed to one of the models on the page and looked up at Marty. It was still a jolt to see her close up, but Marty met her gaze, trying to keep her eyes from wandering over the young woman's patched-up face.

"That's a real pretty dress, Ludie. Would you like to order it?"

"Na. Na." Ludie shook her head hard, tapping with her finger on the model's face.

"The girl? You want to order the girl? That's not a doll, Ludie." Marty paused, then spoke again, louder, separating the words, as if talking to a child, or a deaf person. "You can't buy her. You can only buy her clothes."

"Na. Na." Ludie's shoulders shook with laughter as she picked up the pad and pencil. "ORDER HER FACE." She showed Marty what she had written, then put down the pad, making a circular motion over her own face.

Marty stared at the writing on the page. Ludie's

printing was fine, much nicer than her own. She had not even imagined the colored woman knew how to write at all. Suddenly she realized with a shock that she had considered Ludie somewhat, well, retarded, as if her brain had been lost as well as her body. She felt ashamed and embarrassed, and it must have shown on her face, for Ludie picked up the tablet and wrote again.

"IT'S O.K. DON'T MIND YOURSELF." When she raised her face, it glowed with sweetness and Marty hardly saw the scars.

Something tugged hard at Marty at that moment, something that made her want to reach out and wrap her arms around the girl next to her, to set aside this time, define it, as the beginning of her feelings of friendship for Ludie.

She stayed awhile longer, helping Ludie to clean the cages and crush more of the yellowroot leaves that Chili said were good for cuts, as well as the tonic Ludie fed her animals to bring them back to health.

When the sun was high and hot, Marty said goodbye, promising to return the following day if she could. As she entered the woods, she had a great desire to pull shut some imaginary door, sealing off this new part of her life.

Many years ago someone in Caldwell had decreed that on Wednesday afternoons a great commercial recess would take place. At least that's what Marty decided that day, watching her uncle nap in the rocking chair beside her. They had come out to the porch after dinner to wait for Aunt Letta, although why it was important to keep this vigil Marty did not understand. All the stores in Caldwell closed at noon on Wednesdays, and Marty imagined their owners rushing home, gulping down their dinners, then flopping on bed, couch, hammock, or rocking chair, getting down to the real business of Wednesdays. It had always been a mystery to her how grown-ups could fall asleep in the middle of the day, and she pondered this question again, watching her uncle snore softly next to her, puffs of air pushing his lips out rhythmically.

She had been full of corn bread and good intentions after dinner. No longer would she deceive Uncle Ray about visiting with Ludie and her family. It bothered her to lie, even though it wasn't actually lying since she had no real reason to believe her aunt and uncle would object to her friendship with the colored girl. Still, some instinct kept her from sharing her experience with them until she was sure.

Well, she had tried. She really had tried to confess everything. Her plan had been to first convince Uncle Ray that Negroes were undeserving of the kind of treatment she had witnessed day before yesterday in Claxton. They were, after all, God's children, the same as anybody. Surely he could see that, and when he did, how could he possibly object to Ludie? With that in mind she had sat next to him on the porch, singing softly as she settled herself in the rocker, "Jesus loves the little children. . . . Red and yellow, black and white, they are precious in his sight. . . ." See, Uncle Ray? All God's children, just like you said. No harm in going to see one of God's children.

"You taking on Aunt Letta's habit, Martha Chafin? Singing yourself to China?"

She had laughed nervously, answering with a shrug. "I don't think I could get all the way to China on that song. Mainly I was remembering a little colored boy I saw in Claxton yesterday." Ask me what happened, Uncle Ray. I promise I won't embarrass you by telling you how sad it made me.

"That so? What'd he do?"

A blue jay's screech from the trees in front had seemed to warn her, but Marty had ignored it. Then, carefully avoiding her own perceptions, she had related the incident of the child at the water fountain.

During the telling, her uncle had looked at her with a puzzled expression on his face, but when she had finished, his features relaxed and he had grinned and wagged his head slowly. "Well, sugah, that li'l fella was just upset 'cause he don't understand things yet. He will when he gets bigger."

"I'm bigger, Uncle Ray, and I don't understand." Okay, here it goes. Help me Uncle Ray. Help me tell you about Ludie.

"What? 'Bout colored people drinking from white fountains?"

She knew he was staring hard at her, and she fastened her eyes to the floor of the porch. "Uh-huh. That, too, but mostly the whole thing about coloreds and white being so . . . so separated 'n all." Tell him, silly. He'll understand. You don't have to beat around the bush with Uncle Ray.

He had risen to sit in front of her on the porch railing. "Looka here, Martha. You ought not be studyin' all that mess. It's just something that goes way back and it ain't gon' change anytime soon." He paused, rubbing a hand over his brow. "See, when one group of people is . . . well, I guess you'd call it 'inferior' "—overhead, the jay squawked again, indignantly—"when one group is inferior, they eventually get to be of a lower class than the other. Happens all the time."

Marty had leaned forward then, letting the air cool her back, damp from the cane of the rocking chair. "So," she had said, "the reason colored people can't associate with whites is because they're not as good as we are?" Red and yellow, black and white . . . they're good enough for Jesus, for Christmas' sakes!

He had smiled patiently at her. "Being good don't have nothin' to do with it. It's just that, intellectually"—the word was drawn out, special emphasis on the third syllable—"they're not up to white folks. They got little brains. Can't think as good. That's all. They can't help it."

"But we can be friends with the nigrahs, can't we?"

She was climbing to some high place—exhilarated, but a bit frightened. "I mean I have friends at home who aren't as smart in school as I am." Friends who aren't as smart as I know Ludie to be, Uncle Ray.

"Martha, darlin'," her uncle said as he pushed his face toward her, staring in vacant amazement. "Playin' with pickaninnies is one thing, but you sure as shootin' don't do no socializing with the coloreds, 'specially not at your age." He had rolled his eyes in disbelief, moving back to sit in the chair beside her. "Why first they'd be friends, then next thing you know they'd be husbands and wives, and it'd end up with nobody having any sense. Surely you can understand that!"

Yes sirree, I do.

Shortly afterward her uncle had fallen asleep, and Marty had pushed their conversation aside and written a letter to Anna Raye.

Now as she sat watching Uncle Ray's peaceful sleep, she was torn between love and loyalty to the dear man next to her and the compelling need to confirm what she sensed: Somehow, long ago, something had gone terribly wrong for colored people.

NINE

Under a sky the color of shirt cardboard, Marty followed Ludie through a path in the brush behind Sister's. Even without the sun the day was uncomfortably warm, and the tiny squirrel wriggling against her chest didn't help. An unexpected gust of air puffed up the musty smell of the dry grass, and Ludie stopped and looked toward the sky.

"Gangh yan."

"Rain?" asked Marty.

Ludie's head bobbed, her mouth pulling slightly to one side in a smile. Marty was pleased each time she was able to interpret Ludie's actions and words. By the end of her second visit, yesterday, she had begun to understand much of what the girl said simply by watching her closely. Actually, it hadn't been too hard getting used to her appearance either, once Marty had gotten to know the person behind the crudely seamed face. If Chili hadn't found her that day, Marty thought, she might have gone on thinking that Ludie was as bad as she looked. That's what a lot of people did—liked or disliked somebody because of how they looked.

The squirrel's claws dug through her blouse. "Ouch, you little dickens. Be still. We'll get you back to your house in a minute." Ludie turned around and held out her arms. "That's all right. I'll keep him," said Marty.

The yellowroot, or whatever herbs Ludie had used on the animal, must have been magic, for by the time Marty had returned yesterday, the furry creature was leaping about in his cage, anxious to return to the woods. They were taking him where Ludie had found him.

Presently the path narrowed, and Marty followed Ludie around a group of young oak trees. As the tree trunks broadened and the undergrowth became less dense, Ludie slowed her pace. Stopping at the base of a good-sized tree, she turned and took the animal from Marty.

"Is this where he was?"

Ludie grunted agreeably and placed the squirrel on

the ground beneath the tree. "Yanh, yanh," she said, giving him a gentle push with her hand. For a brief second the squirrel looked back at Ludie with his raisin eyes, as if thanking her, then with a snap of his head turned and scampered up the tree.

Back at Sister's Chili stood over a pot, stirring with a big stick. He looked up as Marty and Ludie entered the yard. "Ludie, tell Mama ain't no sense washin' when we can't hang." He sounded like any little brother asking an older sister to intercede.

"Gangh yan," Ludie called to her mother.

Sister was stringing rope at the side of the porch, twisting it around hooks on the posts. "Rain or what-all, we gon' git sheets dried fo' Miss Julia. You jes' rinch 'em, 'n brang 'em on up heah, boy."

"Let me help, Sister," Marty said, bolting up the back steps and picking up a piece of rope.

"Sweet chile. Jes' you holt ont' dis piece o' rope whilst I draws it tight." The colored woman wore a shapeless print dress whose sleeves had been ripped out, and as she twisted the rope into place, the dark flab of her arms rippled like chocolate pudding.

As she held the rope, Marty squinted to see the inside of the house through the darkness of the screen door. A wave of heat came from inside, and Marty could see a wood stove like the one her aunt had owned before she had redone the kitchen. Something on the stove filled the air with a steamy vegetable smell; crowder or black-eyed peas. She could make out a table at one side, and a few more pieces of furniture, but the shadowy screen made it impossible to see any more. When Sister had secured the rope, Marty went to join Ludie at the well.

Gazing down into the long tunnel of darkness, Marty watched the bucket bring up the cool water, the wheel squeaking it on its way. Ludie lifted the pail to one side and set it down, and Marty looked inside at the clear water magnifying the dents in the bucket's sides. Suddenly she was very thirsty. Ludie dipped a cup into the bucket and pushed it toward her.

"Nngwah?"

The scene at the water fountain flashed in Marty's mind. Now, she thought, now she could test the truth of her feelings—give life to her new ideas. She *wasn't* afraid to drink after colored people. "Nngwah? Ma-anh nngwah?" Ludie repeated.

Boldly Marty took the cup from Ludie, but as it got closer to her lips, she hesitated. Then she drank, water trickling down her chin and onto her blouse. It was hard to drink when your mouth never touched the cup. Ashamed, she passed the cup to Ludie, who to her surprise was snickering behind her hand. The colored girl took a drink, then motioned to Marty to follow her in the house.

Inside, Marty realized that it had not been the screen door that had made the inside of the house seem so dark; it was lack of light. The lone window in that part of the house provided a meager brightness on such a cloudy day.

Marty sat on a wooden chair, its seat made from straps of leather woven together, and waited for Ludie, who had gone into the other section of the house. A fireplace in the center of the cabin divided the living area in the front from the kitchen. By craning her head Marty was able to see the other part of the house from her place near the kitchen table. There was an iron bed, with a wooden box that served as a table, against one wall. Across from this, on the opposite wall, was a seat that had come from the front of a car, and next to that Marty recognized an old table of Aunt Letta's. In the kitchen a cot had been placed near the back door, and under the window was a metal stand with a basin on it. It wasn't so much the shabbiness of the house's furnishings that struck Marty as it was the lack of anything but the most utilitarian.

As she waited, a kind of coldness spread over her. Not the fear kind of cold, but something else, a not-belonging, lonely kind of cold. All at once the smell of the vegetables cooking caused her stomach to slide. She wished Ludie would hurry with whatever she was doing.

The floor in the front of the house creaked, and Ludie came into the kitchen, pressing to her bosom the tablet of paper Marty had seen yesterday. With her head she gestured toward the door, and Marty followed her out to the back porch and sat next to her.

Ludie took a pencil from her pocket and wrote on the tablet. "TOO HOT INSIDE." The tail of the final *e* curled gracefully, and Marty was again impressed with the excellence of Ludie's handwriting.

"You sure write good, Ludie."

"Yanh." The pencil spoke then. "WHEN YOU GO HOME?"

Marty was disappointed. Obviously she had over-stayed her welcome. She stood up, squaring her shoulders. "I'm going right now. I have some things to do before dinner."

Ludie frowned, puzzled, then giggled, shaking her head. "Nanh, nanh." The dark knobby hand tugged at Martha's shorts, and Marty sat back down cautiously.

"WHEN YOU GO BACK TO CITY?" poured swiftly and beautifully onto the page.

"Ohhh," Marty said, relieved. "Probably sometime next week when Mama and Daddy come to get me."

"I DON'T WANT YOU TO GO. I WILL MISS YOU. I LIKE YOU."

Marty felt warm inside. She could not remember ever hearing those words from a friend. Oh, sure, she could always tell, by the way they acted, if people liked her or not, but nobody had ever just come right out and said it to her before. She liked it. It made her feel really good, and very close to the girl beside her. The blue eyes held the brown, and Marty knew that something greater than a look had passed between them. "I like you, too, Ludie, and I'm gonna miss you, but . . ." Suddenly she felt uncomfortable. "But, well, Daddy has to be back at work, and—" She hesitated, then turned quickly to Ludie. "Did you know my daddy when he lived in Caldwell?"

Ludie wagged her head, then wrote, "HE LEAVE WHEN I SMALL."

"But my uncle Lonnie, his baby brother? Did you know him?" Maybe they had played together like her and Jun Reid.

An eerie, wild look widened Ludie's eyes before she looked away from Marty. Minutes passed before Ludie wrote again. "YOU COME TOMORROW?"

Marty nearly asked Ludie about her uncle Lonnie again, thinking perhaps she hadn't heard, but instead she nodded her head and told her she would try to come tomorrow.

Ludie probably wouldn't have remembered Uncle Lonnie anyway, Marty thought as she passed beneath the first tall trees at the edge of the woods. After all, he had been sent to a military school when he was twelve, and after that he had gone on to college.

When Marty crossed the highway and started up the lane, she peered hard at the house. "Thad?" she said aloud. What in the world was Thad doing sitting on Aunt Letta's front steps? She sensed trouble, and watched uneasily, with steps slowed, as the boy came out to meet her.

"Where all them tadpoles you told Miss Letta you went to get, Martha?"

So. The third degree was to come from Thad. "I had lots, but I dropped the jar. On a rock. It was slippery down there."

"Hunh," he said sarcastically.

She ignored Thad's response. "What are you doin' at Aunt Letta's, anyway?"

The clump of hair fell over his forehead and he swatted at it. "Bigmama's got one of her headaches from all the dust yesterday, so I'm eatin' with y'all. Miss Letta invited me."

"How long have you been waiting on the porch?"

"Pretty long." She could feel his eyes on her. "Longer than it takes to get a jar of tadpoles."

"Well, it's too bad I dropped 'em, that's all. I had some nice ones. Some almost frogs, and little biddy ones too." It was amazing how easy the words came.

"Yeah, I just bet. You musta had a hard time gettin' to the creek through the woods though, 's all I got to say."

Marty came to a full stop and put her hands on her hips. She jutted her head forward, staring hard at Thad. "Why are you talking like this, Thad? Like you don't believe I went to the creek at all?"

Thad kicked at a rock in the lane and looked back toward the smoke suspended over Sister's. "If you said you were down there, I guess you were, but you ain't never gone by yourself. Without me. Somethin' else too." Thad started to walk again, and Marty followed. "It waddn't jes' today you went off by yourself for a long time."

"So? I'm nearly thirteen. I don't have to have a baby-sitter."

"I think you went back to Sister's to spy some more." He spoke quickly, in a hurry to relieve himself of the words, then took a deep breath.

Marty almost blurted out everything at that moment, but something pulled her back. She still had not made up her mind to confide in anyone. "That's stupid, for Christmas' sakes. Let's hurry up and go eat."

Uncle Ray's truck turned in behind them as they crossed the yard to the house, and Marty ran to greet him.

"What you two young'uns up to?" His face had the "I got a secret" sparkle.

"Uncle Ray, we sure would like you to take us into Claxton to see the Tarzan movie." Not that she liked Tarzan movies all that much, but it was something to do, and might take Thad's mind off Sister and Ludie. She hooked her arm through her uncle's as they climbed the steps.

"Have to be tomorrow, sugah. Even though it is against her religion to go to Claxton on a Friday afternoon, Letta's goin' in to get her hair fixed, and she'll take y'all. C'mon. I smell Thelma's good chicken pie."

"We fixin' to get a gullywasher," said Aunt Letta, pulling her hand through the pile of black-eyed peas in the newspaper in her lap. The hulls the vegetables had worn lay in a heap between her and Marty, who sat at her aunt's feet on the floor of the porch, next to Thad. The youngsters shared a newspaper that held a scant cup of the tiny, kidney-shaped pellets. Although she considered shelling peas the boringest job in the world, Marty had agreed to earn a ride to the movies tomorrow by helping Aunt Letta get them ready to can. At first she had tried to keep up with her aunt, running her thumbnail up the slender knobby pods and spilling the peas onto the paper, but after a while the wet membrane from the shell began to sting and burn under her fingernail, so she used a less painful but slower method. She glanced at Thad, who was tearing at the shells clumsily.

"Looks like it might be rainin' over yonder already." Aunt Letta pushed her fleshy finger out. "I speck we'll be able to finish shellin' out here before it gets us, though." She looked down at the peas on Marty's paper. "If—If, that is, y'all shell faster. I declare." She paused, chuckling. "That little pile of peas ain't never gon' get y'all to Claxton."

"Aunt Letta. You know that girl, Sister's girl, that comes to bring the sheets?" Marty was aware of Thad's head jerking up sharply.

"Ludie?"

"Yes'm. Thelma said she got burned in a fire when she was small."

"Uh-huh. She did, but she waddn't all that small. She was 'bout your age when it happened."

"How did it happen? The fire?"

"Martha," Thad said urgently, "you better hush talkin' so much and get to shellin'."

Marty gave an exasperated whimper. "I can talk and shell, too, Thad Walcott. Besides, I'm keeping up with you." She turned back to her aunt. "How did the fire happen that burned her, Aunt Letta?"

Her aunt reached for another handful of peas from the hamper, then sat back and began rocking slowly. The mounds of bosom heaved in a deep sigh. "I just don't remember too much at all about that, honey, to tell the truth. Just somethin' that happened, 's all it was, 'bout seven or eight years ago."

A rush of cool air lifted the edge of the newspaper next to Marty, and she glanced up. The tops of the pecan trees were bending, left, then right. Aunt Letta noticed, too, and gathered her pea-filled paper in her arms. "Come on, chilluns, we better move our business to the kitchen, or we gon' get wet."

After supper Marty lay across her bed listening to the gentle rap of rain on the roof. Nancy Drew lay open beside her, but she had stopped reading *The Mystery at the Moss-Covered Mansion* some time ago. She was thinking of Ludie and of her first impressions of her. There had been the grotesque hag, then the simpleminded, childlike creature; how wrong to think Ludie retarded because she couldn't speak. Marty smiled, conjuring up her new image of Ludie—cheerful, bright, industrious Ludie, no longer feared or pitied but loved.

She rose and walked to the window, staring out at the wet blackness and the network of raindrops chasing each other down the pane. Whatever the reason for the tug from the cabin across the woods, her feelings were real, and Marty knew she would steal away again in the morning, and the next and the next, for as long as it took to discover all she needed to know about Ludie.

TEN

You better take your linen bolero to wear case it's cold in there."

The peal of Aunt Letta's voice swung mockingly over Marty's head as she sat shivering in the air-conditioned movie theater. She had been hot when they had left Caldwell, and the thought of wearing any more clothes had made her sting all over. Even when they stood outside the movie theater and she saw the blue banner with the white, snow-dripping letters that spelled out AIR CONDITIONED INSIDE, she was glad she had not taken the jacket, glad she had worn her sundress with more of herself to get cooled by the frosty blasts she knew were awaiting her and Thad. But now. Oh, now. She wished she could wrap herself in the wall of wine-colored velvet covering the movie screen. They still would have to wait thirty minutes before the picture started, since they had had to come early because of her aunt's beauty parlor appointment.

Marty had been so excited when she had returned from Ludie's that she had nearly forgotten she and Thad were going to the movie this afternoon. She had run all the way home, hugging the precious sheets of brown paper Ludie had given her, eager to share her latest discovery with—with whom? Well, she hadn't exactly made up her mind until she had seen Thad standing on Miss Julia's steps in his starched khaki pants and his hair all watered down. Then she had remembered about the movie, and at the same time had decided to share her secret with him. Everything seemed to be working out too. Thirty minutes was enough for them to have a really good talk.

She huddled against the back of the seat, trying to think of a way to begin. Should she tell him everything, from the beginning? About going to Ludie's every day, or just about today, or—

"What'd you bring home from Sister's? Those brown papers?" Thad spoke straight ahead, to the curtains on the stage.

"How do you know where I got 'em?" she replied in a whisper.

"Because. I just do," Thad whispered back. Then, after looking around the empty theater, he raised his voice slightly. "I followed you when you followed Ludie after she brought Bigmama's laundry this morning."

Marty slumped back, the horsehair covering of the seat itchy against her bare back. So, he knew. She had planned to tell him anyway; it was just that his knowing, even the slightest scrap, took some of the excitement away. "Well," she began, "if I tell you, you have to promise to God and hope to die not to tell Aunt Letta and Uncle Ray." She glanced quickly toward the front of the theater, then back at Thad. "I'm going to tell them. I really am, but just not right now. Promise?"

"What for? I know for sure you went over there this morning, and probably every other morning, too, since the time we went together. So what's to promise about?" Thad's eyes had that haughty glaze they got sometimes.

" 'Cause there's more to it, Mr. Smarty, than just going over there. Now will you promise? Because if you don't, I won't tell you about the most special part; what happened this morning." She folded her arms across her chest and watched him, hoping his curiosity would override his stubbornness. She sure wanted to talk to somebody. Almost a full minute went by before he spoke.

"Awww, all right." The green eyes narrowed, looking at her sideways. "But it better be worth it."

For the next quarter hour words tumbled from Marty's mouth like gems from a pouch. From time to time she checked Thad's face for some sign, some indication, that he was catching her enthusiasm as she described her initial visit with Chili, and Ludie, the explanation of the caged animals, Ludie's cleverness with the herbs, and her artistic handwriting. She told him everything, laying before him a day-by-day log of her relationship with Ludie and her family. If Thad was impressed, he didn't show it. When she began the account of her most recent visit, that morning, she hesitated.

How could she tell Thad what she had learned from Sister about the fire that had brought so much misfortune to Ludie? About how a white college boy had "put a baby in her," and when he had learned of Ludie's condition, how he had become enraged, knocking her down and leaving her unconscious in the cabin. Sister had said nobody knew for sure whether a pan of grease on the stove had caught fire or if the boy had started the blaze deliberately.

Anyway, she had no intention of talking about anything of a sexual nature with Thad. She decided to skip that part and moved along to the business of the brown papers.

"So," she continued breathlessly, "you were right

about this morning. I did follow Ludie back, and caught up with her about halfway. She told me she had something to show me when we got to her house."

"What do you mean, she *told* you? You can't make any sense of all that 'yanh yanh yanh' stuff."

Marty paraphrased Chili's words: "If you're around her enough, you can understand her. Anyway, when we got to the house she brought out a picture she had drawn on brown paper. It was a picture of me, holding the squirrel we took to the woods. The one I just told you about? I know she didn't draw it when I was there, so that means she remembered everything about me. Like what I had on, and my hair and everything, to be able to draw it." She turned to Thad, triumphant. "So what do you think about that?"

She was pleased to see the hardness slip from his face and a glint of interest stir behind the long, dark eyelashes.

"Was the drawing any good?"

She plunged through the opening. "Better than Mrs. Johnson, my art teacher, and she draws for a living. Mama even bought one of her paintings for one hundred dollars, and Ludie's ten times better."

"I guess you really know a lot about art, too, huh?" Thad said with a sneer. He was trying to hold on to his indifference, but Marty knew she had struck pay dirt.

"Listen. Anybody in their right mind can see they're good." Her mind began pushing ideas out of her mouth. "I'm going to show some to Uncle Ray, and maybe he'll put some in his store to sell; then I'm going to take one to Mrs. Johnson when I get back, and show her, and then—well, who knows what could happen. If Ludie sells enough . . . Gosh, Thad, maybe she could get an operation to make her talk, and get to be a famous artist or something, and then—"

"Marty." Thad spoke quietly but urgently, looking around as people began dribbling into the theater. "Don't talk so loud, for gosh sakes. Besides, when you tell Mr. and Mrs. Armstrong about those pictures, they're gonna know right off you been hanging around at Sister's, and they're not gonna like it one bit."

"But see, I figure when he sees how good Ludie's drawings are, Uncle Ray won't care. He told me once about how colored people have smaller brains and all? Well, when he sees how smart Ludie is, he'll—"

"That is absolutely ridiculous." Thad sounded at least thirty years old.

Marty raised her eyes to his face, to see if it matched his voice; if by some chance he had become grown up in an instant. Thad the boy still sat beside her. His lips were pressed tightly together, and his eyes darted about the movie theater as though he were struggling to keep some ancient sadness from escaping through his features.

"Why do you say it's ridiculous?" she asked. "Why, as soon as Uncle Ray sees—"

"You still don't get it, do you?" he interrupted

fiercely. "You can't tell anybody down here what you just told me, about Ludie 'n all. Most of all, you can't let 'em find out you been over there so much, especially with Chili around. That can get you in a heap o' trouble, Martha Chafin."

"But what about Ludie? She could be famous, and talk maybe—"

"And that's another thing. Ludie won't ever be famous. Not if she's the best artist in the world." He began speaking rapidly, as if his nerve might fail him at any moment. "Ludie's a colored and always will be. She'll never, ever be nothing but a nigger! That's all people see. Not if she's smart, or draws good, or anything, just that she's a nigger. And if you don't want to get hurt bad, you'll forget about doing anything about her stupid pictures." He sat back, breathing hard. Marty had never seen Thad show so much emotion. She was almost embarrassed for him.

They sat silently for the next few minutes, the space between them still charged with the energy of Thad's outburst. Marty was confused. Thad had seemed so angry at the hopelessness of helping Ludie. Like it wasn't fair that her talent would never be recognized. But then, she asked herself, why did he join in with Janelle last Sunday, laughing at me when I said Jun was my friend, and why did he side with Janelle about Negroes being like animals, apes?

Gradually a thin line of light began to widen in

Marty's mind, and when it had spread, great and bright, she turned to him.

"Last Sunday when you and Janelle were making fun of coloreds, calling them apes 'n all . . ."

"What about it?"

"You just went along with her 'cause you were afraid."

"Huh. Afraid of that ol' cruddy girl?"

"Not her, maybe, but what she might tell her brothers. That maybe you were a nigger lover, and that'd be about the worst thing to be down here, I guess. And that's why you told me never to talk about how I feel, too, iddn't it?"

"You think you know it all, don't you?" His voice was a sneer as he carefully peeled back the paper from a square of nut-flavored caramel.

"Not all, but some. I think I just figured out that you might feel just the same as I do about the colored people."

"Oh, is that right? And how do *we* feel, Miss Armstrong with all the answers?"

She wasn't going to allow his sarcasm to interfere with her opportunity to give life to the ideas her mind had collected over the past week. "That Negroes are just as smart, as clean, and work just as hard as whites, and that there should be no separate drinking fountains, or bus depots, or restaurants, or any of the everyday things whites take for granted. They shouldn't have to think about where they eat or drink or go to school, or have to hide talent under a basket of dirty laundry just because their skin's a different color. That's what I think, and I believe you do, too, *Mister* Walcott." It was Marty's turn to breathe heavily now, as her mind turned over and over. How long had these thoughts been lying there? Probably since before her coming to Caldwell. What had made them pop up now, like green shoots at the sun? She was sure it wasn't some stage or growing-up phase she was going through. Now that her feelings had become words, written on someone else's mind, she could see them clearly and they couldn't be denied.

"Well, anyway, it don't matter how you, we, feel." Thad's right foot beat a stacatto under the seat ahead. "It don't matter what anybody thinks, not even my father, and he tried too. If you don't want something bad to happen to you down here, you'll pretend you think like they do, whether it's right or not."

"Your father? Did you say your father? What about . . ." Marty had to push back to let two people cross in front of them.

"Nothin' 'bout him," he whispered as the curtains parted and the voice of Lowell Thomas boomed from the screen.

Marty forgot about Thad, about his father, and about Ludie while Tarzan swung, wrestled an alligator, stopped a thundering elephant herd, and rescued Boy from the sacrificial altar of the Temple of the Unknown God. Just once, though, she would have liked to see Tarzan in a passionate love scene with Jane.

The heat of the afternoon enveloped them as they came out of the theater. Marty didn't mind. It felt good after the biting cold inside. Her eyes searched the street for her aunt's car.

"You got money left?" Thad asked her.

"Twenty-five cents."

"They're selling snow cones down yonder. I'll go get us two if you'll watch for Miz Armstrong."

She thought for a minute. A snow cone was the last thing she wanted after being so cold, but the candy had made her thirsty. "Okay," she replied, fishing the money from her purse.

As she watched him walk away, she recalled their conversation in the theater. What had he meant about his father? She was sure he had been going to tell her when the film started, but she knew better than to bring it up in front of Aunt Letta. She remembered the tremor in his voice as he warned about her friendship with Ludie, like he was afraid. She lifted her chin. No need to be afraid, she thought. Most I'll get if Uncle Ray doesn't approve is a good talking to.

A horn blared through her thoughts, and she looked up to see her aunt's head peeking over the top of the steering wheel of the Ford. She waved to Aunt Letta and strained her eyes up the street for Thad. Presently she caught sight of him walking fast, holding the two red-topped cones out in front. She ran to meet him.

"Take it quick, 'cause it's starting to melt," he said, handing her one.

"Aunt Letta must have gone around the block. She was here a minute ago." Marty licked the sweet cherry juice rapidly to stop the dripping, then sucked at the ice around the edge until it was clear. Another toot of the horn and the car reappeared and stopped.

"Aunt Letta! You got a permanent wave," said Marty, slamming the car door. Her aunt's neck was still red, and her hair sat in small tubes all over her head.

"Sho' did. That Toni I gave myself a couple of months ago just didn't hold up, so I decided to splurge. Now, how'd y'all like the picture show?"

"It was real good, Miss Letta. Thanks for taking me," Thad said between slurps from the backseat.

"See"—Marty turned to her aunt—"some crooks had stolen the precious stones. Rubies, I believe, out of the idol's eyes? And the natives went around killing everybody until Tarzan got the stones back."

"Martha, you had your hands in front of your face nearly the whole time. How'd you see all that?"

"I did not, Thad. Just at the scary parts 's all. Who wants to see people gettin' stuck with spears?"

"Well," said her aunt, "give me a good love story any day. Ray, now. He likes all them war pictures and murder stories, but there's enough of that in the real world without somebody making it up and showin' off with it."

After that the journey to Claxton continued in silence until they turned from the state highway.

"Wonder what Ray's doing home this time o' day?" remarked Aunt Letta. "It's not even four o'clock, for goodness' sakes."

They could see the truck in the driveway as they turned toward the house.

When she got out of the car, Marty noticed her uncle standing just inside the screen door. He opened the door and stood silently on the porch, his face stern, almost sour, as he watched Marty approach behind Thad and her aunt.

"Thad, you better run on home. Martha's got to come inside now." Those were the first words out of his mouth—not "hello," not "how was the picture show?" Nothing.

Thad shot Marty a worried glance, then went across the yard.

"What is it, Ray? What's wrong?" Aunt Letta looked up from the bottom step at her husband.

"Never mind. Y'all come on in. We've got some serious family business to discuss." Uncle Ray held the door, and Marty was sure he could hear her heart thump as she passed by him.

ELEVEN

All Marty's bravado about facing a lecture from her uncle remained on the front porch, and when she entered the house her hands were clammy.

"Come sit here, sugah, next to your ol' Uncle Ray." To her surprise her uncle's dark eyes were smiling as he motioned for her to sit next to him on the sofa.

She sat, her eyes on his face, and he put an arm about her, drawing her close. Gradually her tension subsided. Maybe this wasn't about her morning excursions after all.

"Martha," he began, "you know your aunt Letta and I love you to death. Why, you're as much ours as you are George and Beth's." He shifted to peer into her face. "You know that, now don't you?"

"Yessir." What in the world?

Aunt Letta sat across the room on the edge of a chair, and when her eyes met Marty's, she shrugged.

"Well," Uncle Ray continued, "when you love somebody as much as we love you, you just naturally want the best for them. You sho' don't wanna see 'em do things that might hurt 'em in the long run. Understand?"

"Yessir, Uncle Ray." Her aunt's swinging foot was fascinating.

"That's why, when I heard how you been spendin' your mornings recently, it like to broke my heart."

"What, Ray? What could the child possibly have been doing to get you so upset, for Lord's sakes?" Aunt Letta stopped her foot action and leaned forward.

Marty saw her uncle put a palm to silence his wife.

"Your daddy and mama expect Letta and me to watch after you good. Now I know you're a big girl, a young lady, and don't need no sugar nanny no more, or have somebody follow you around, but for your own good you got to realize that there's certain places a nice girl don't go, certain things that decent young ladies don't do!" He leaned out, gripping his left ankle, which lay across his right knee. "What you do when you're in Augusta is your mama and daddy's concern, but when you're down here, you have to behave and act how *we* expect you to."

Marty continued listening silently, no longer fearful, but for the first time she could remember, anger at her uncle began to rise like hot liquid within her. Treating her like a baby. "Decent young ladies," like she wasn't, like she was some low-class trash. Behave yourself, as if she were doing something awful, for Christmas' sakes. She hadn't done anything bad. Nothing bad at all! Uncle Ray was wrong, and she'd show him how wrong he was!

"Martha!" Aunt Letta called. "Listen to Uncle Ray now, so we can find out what this is all about."

"Martha knows what it's about. You want to tell your aunt Letta where you been running off to every morning this week?"

Marty remained silent, her voice unable to get past the fiery coal of anger lodged in her throat.

"Well, I can imagine you wouldn't want to talk about it much." Uncle Ray got up, pulled his tobacco pouch from his pocket and began filling his pipe. It seemed a week passed before he lit the pipe and drew on its stem. He faced his wife. "Letta, seems like we were right about Martha Chafin growing up fast. Seems like she's outgrown all her little girl and boy playmates down here and prefers the company of older boys. One in particular."

What was he talking about now?

"Jewel? She's been running off to see Jewel Turner every day?" asked Aunt Letta.

"Hunh," grunted Ray Armstrong. "Right now I'd

almost be glad to settle for Jewel—be more natural anyway."

Marty sat back against the cushions, watching her uncle walk back and forth across the room. This whole business had taken such an unexpected turn, she was anxious to see how it would end.

"No, Letta. Martha was a little feisty last Saturday because I wouldn't let her see Jun when we went out to Cole's." He nodded, gesturing toward his wife with his pipe. "You know, we discussed all that." Aunt Letta nodded back. "Well, it seems Martha went and found herself another colored . . . friend." He stopped pacing and stood in front of Marty, staring down at her. She returned his gaze as if he were a stranger telling an interesting story. "Martha's been spending the last several mornings over yonder with Chili, Sister's boy." The fuse lit, Uncle Ray pulled his cold black eyes from Marty's and stood back.

"Chili?" Aunt Letta clasped a palm to her bosom and fell back against the chair. "Oh my law-ud! Not again!"

"Chili?!" screeched Marty. "Who told you that, Uncle Ray? Who told you all this stuff?"

"Who told don't matter a iota now. My information came from a reliable source—even came to the store to tell me so it wouldn't get on the party line. Can you deny you seen that colored boy every day this week? Can you? I want to hear it from your own mouth!"

"Well, yes, I've seen Chili some, but—"

Uncle Ray shook his head sadly and walked to the window behind his wife.

Aunt Letta was writhing in her chair, her hand at her head. "Oh, when I think what might have happened." She pulled herself up abruptly, terror on her face. "Did it? Did anything happen, Martha?"

"Now just a minute! Y'all must have just about the evilest minds in the world!" Marty cried, drawing herself up as tall as she could. She didn't know what she was going to say, exactly, but, well, if it was some crazy mixed-up tale they wanted, she would sure do her part to please them. "I guess it's not important who you talked to about me, but you could have asked me before taking somebody else's word that I was up to something bad." She felt her eyes begin to fill and she pushed back the tears. "Chili didn't have anything to do with the reason I've been 'running off,' as you call it."

"Sugah, don't make it worse by telling more stories," said her uncle, all wise and pious-looking from his place near the window.

"Okay. You want to know the real reason I went off every day? Well, I'll tell you!" Her face was getting hot. "It was gonna be a surprise for y'all." She looked from one to the other, nodding rapidly. "That's right. A surprise. Something nice, just for my family. Something I thought would make you happy." She stopped. Now it was her turn to light the fuse. "I've been 'running off' to the woods to draw animals. Birds, and wildlife, and things I don't see much at home." Aunt Letta looked at her husband liked he'd stomped on a baby chick.

"That's all I've been doing," Marty continued. "And y'all have spoiled everything! Making something dirty out of it!" Tears sprang to her eyes, then spilled over her cheeks. She brushed at them, snuffling loudly. She was angry and hurt at what they'd believed about her, and angry and ashamed at herself for compounding the lie, but she couldn't have told them anything else. Not yet. They had given up their right to hear the truth by so readily believing the worst. If it came out different from the way it was, it was their own fault. She hadn't wanted to lie. She hadn't. But they would have messed up the truth.

Aunt Letta was on her feet at once, with her arms around Marty. "Darlin', Uncle Ray didn't know." She patted Marty's back softly and stroked her hair. "Ray, she's been drawin' pictures, for heaven's sakes."

Cautiously Marty raised one wet eye to see her uncle's face. Just for an instant it seemed to melt, but as if he sensed he was losing control, he stiffened his features again. "Well, then, how 'bout lettin' us see some of these pictures you say you been drawin' on?"

Pulling away from her aunt, Marty wiped her eyes with the back of her hand. "All right, I'll go get them. Maybe you won't think they're any good though."

All the way into her bedroom her thoughts were jumping over one another. What had she started? What if they made her draw something in front of them? Suppose they even knew that Ludie could draw? She could hear them murmuring in the livingroom as she knelt at the edge of her bed and withdrew the sheets of brown paper, selecting three, leaving the one of herself.

Well, it was too late to turn back now. "Oh, God," she whispered to the ceiling. "I'm sorry about all this, and if I ever get out of this mess, I promise I won't lie about anything, ever again. Amen."

In the livingroom she spread the sheets over the sofa and stood back, clasping and unclasping her hands. Her uncle walked back and forth, pulling on his pipe, not speaking. Next to Marty her aunt Letta held a puffy palm against each cheek, letting her eyes trail over the pictures. She didn't speak either, and their silence was causing a knot to form in Marty's stomach.

Then finally, "I don't know 'bout you, Ray, but I think we got ourselves a mighty talented little gal." Marty exhaled.

"I tell you what's true, sugah pie." Uncle Ray's eyes, so cold only moments before, now were bright. "You sho' put one ovuh on Uncle Ray. I may not know jack about art 'n stuff, but they look right good to me. Why, this squirrel looks real enough to run right off the page, don't it, Letta?"

"For the world," Aunt Letta replied, triumphant.

"Do you really like them?" Marty asked, finding her voice. "I'll be getting into more advanced art next year, and maybe I can do better." Oh, just keep quiet. Don't keep putting bricks in that big wall of lies.

"Don't see how they can be a whole lot better, but I know one thing, Mr. Raymond Armstrong." Aunt Letta had her hands on her hips, glaring at her husband. "You better tell that certain party they were barking up the wrong tree with all their 'reliable' information!"

"Miss Letta." It was Thelma, standing in the door. "I tak'n them vegetables and made some soup for yo's supper, and put the rest in mah take-home jar."

Marty's aunt jiggled happily. "That's fine. Come on in here and see the art show, Thelma. See what Martha's been doing."

Marty felt the floor move as Thelma lumbered over to the sofa. She had an anxious moment as she watched the big Negro woman's eyes flash with something like recognition, but when Thelma turned, looking down from the mountain of herself, her face showed nothing. "They be fine." The wiry head nodded. "They be jes' fine, Miss."

All at once the weight of what she had done, the sneaking off to Ludie's, the lies, pressed against her, and Marty was certain her shame was visible to everyone in the room. She scooped up the drawings and, keeping her face down, rushed from the room.

Later that evening Uncle Ray suggested they take a ride out to the Dairy Bar and get an ice cream, but Marty said she didn't want to go anywhere. Then he tried to interest her in a game of Parcheesi, and even Monopoly, which she knew he never liked to play because it took so long. It was obvious to Marty that her uncle was trying hard to make up for his accusations of the afternoon, and she also realized that he probably thought her indifference to him meant that she was still pouting. If only she could tell him the real reason for her moodiness. Finally she picked up *The Mystery at the Moss-Covered Mansion* and went to her room.

She had barely crawled up on the bed when she heard the voice of her aunt speaking softly (well, as softly as possible for Aunt Letta) on the other side of the wall.

"Why didn't you just come out and say you were sorry, Raymond? You know that's all the child wants to hear."

"Letta"—her uncle's voice was low, but forceful—"I didn't do nothing to be sorry for. It wasn't me made the mistake, it was Miss Julia, dadgum it!"

"I know, but Martha heard it from you. You need to find some way to make it up to her, bless her heart."

There was a long silence before her uncle spoke. "What do you really think about those drawin's of hers? You know more about that kind of thing than I do. When you went up to Atlanta that time with the church ladies, did y'all see anything that good in that art gallery?"

"Well, certainly, Ray. They's all kinds of famous artists' pictures up there, but a twelve-year-old child can't be put in the same class with them!"

"Okay, then. Let me ask you this. If you saw one of them pictures, framed up, in a store, would you buy it? Even if you didn't know it was Martha had done it?"

"Probably. If there wasn't nothing better I liked, but you got to remember . . ." Marty heard her aunt inhale. "Ray, you ol' devil! I know what you're up to. You gon' take those pictures of Martha's to the store and try to sell 'em for her, aren't you?"

Marty felt her stomach turn completely over, and she held her breath, waiting for her uncle's reply.

"Been stewin' about it. Just wanted to see what you had to say."

Marty stopped listening then in order to deal with the turmoil in her head. Wasn't this what she had planned? To get Ludie's pictures where everybody could see how good they were? Maybe buy them and make her famous, and get an operation so she could talk, 'n all? Wasn't that what she had hoped for all along? Then what was the problem? "Be sure your sins will find you out" . . . was the problem.

She breathed deeply and scrambled across the bed. She would go to them, right now, confess the whole lie, from beginning to end. After all, even if they got horribly mad at her, wouldn't it be a small price to pay if it meant a chance for Ludie? Marty crossed to the door, put her hand on the knob. Then she let it drop. Suppose something else happened? Suppose her uncle became so mad at her because she had lied that he wouldn't show Ludie's pictures anyway?

No, she decided. Her confession right now might not accomplish anything. Oh! If only there were somebody she could talk to right this minute about all of this! Suddenly it came to her, and squaring her shoulders, she walked slowly and deliberately to the side of the bed and knelt beside it.

"Listen here, God," she began softly. "I mean, that is, if you're still listening to me after everything I've done. Remember about 'casting our burdens upon You?' I don't know who said it, but I know you must have told them to, or it wouldn't be in your Word. Anyway, I've made a kind of a mess of things, and I just purely don't know what to do about it, so I'm casting, right now. I hate to do this to you, but I don't know anybody else I can give it to, and you've worked out a lot harder things for other people, I know. Maybe it won't be as hard from up there as it is right down here in the middle of it all. Just try, okay? I'd really appreciate it. Amen."

TWELVE

"Martha? You 'wake?" Aunt Letta chirped softly outside the bedroom door.

Moments before, Marty had heard her uncle's truck rattle down the driveway beneath her window. She sat up, rubbing her eyes. "Yes'm, come on in."

Her aunt's body was wrapped from head to toe in large rayon hyacinths, and her eyes danced as if she had just hidden the golden Easter egg and was dying to tell where it was. She walked to the bed and sat down, pulling the brightly colored duster around her. The hair net she always slept in was still covering her head, so Marty knew her aunt had not been up too long herself. "Martha, darlin'," she began, taking Marty's hand and patting it. "Your uncle Ray's one of the finest, best men, in the world, but there never was but one man completely perfect. You know who that was."

"Jesus."

The hair net bobbed. "Anyway, as good as Ray is, he does make mistakes sometimes, and he knows now he made one when he said those things to you yesterday." The bed bounced as she shifted her round hips to face Marty. "Now, while he might have a hard time saying he's sorry, Ray finds other ways to apologize."

Marty shook her head. "Uncle Ray doesn't need to say anything, Aunt Letta. I could tell he felt bad."

"I know." Her aunt's hand patted out each word on Marty's hand. "Still an' all, that ain't good enough for your uncle Ray. He wants to make it up to you real good." The little gray eyes were bright with the urge to reveal the hiding place of the golden egg. Marty kept her face blank, as if she hadn't heard their conversation the evening before. "The thing is," her aunt continued, "Uncle Ray thinks your drawings might be good enough to sell." Marty drew in her breath to speak. "Now listen, sugah. Ray wants you to take your pictures to the store, to just see how they do. And something else. He knows the Campbell's Soup man that's been coming to the store for years, from

Atlanta? His sister-in-law up there has this kind of gift shop, and Uncle Ray says if your drawings do good down here, why he might give some to the Campbell's man to take to his sister-in-law's shop!" She pulled back, grinning from ear to ear. " 'Course now, if those things start selling like hotcakes, you may end up drawing a lot more than you wanted to, but it might mean something big for you one day." Her aunt stood up, obviously as pleased with herself as if she had produced not only the golden egg but the bird that had laid it as well.

Marty hoped she looked surprised. (Well, the part about the Atlanta gift shop *was* new.) "Oh, Aunt Letta. That's really nice of Uncle Ray. He didn't have to do that." Marty got up and walked to the end of the bed, holding on to the bedpost. "I'm sure I could do more pictures, too, if they did start to sell good." It shouldn't take Ludie long to make more, and when the demand for the pictures had grown, who would care who had really drawn them, anyway? She was back to her original logic, and it suited just fine.

"Well," her aunt said from the doorway, "you get on your clothes and have some breakfast, then carry the pictures down to the store and help Uncle Ray set 'em up so people can see 'em, hear?"

An hour later Marty stepped from the lawn to the dusty, copper road in front of the house, carrying the precious pictures. The powdery dirt of the road slipped between the straps of her sandals, and she stopped in front of Miss Julia's to shake it out, holding the roll of pictures to one side.

She heard the whine of Miss Julia's screen door and looked up to see Thad standing on the porch. "Hey, wait a minute, Martha. I'm coming too."

Not now, she thought, her mind buzzing like the June bugs in the sun-washed field across the road. He's just going to want to know all about yesterday, and I don't feel like talking about it anymore. She had almost justified the lie (okay, the lies) she had told the day before, and she didn't need Thad punching holes in her comfortable conscience.

Thad knelt in the yard, tying his shoes. "Well, come on, Thad. My uncle Ray's waiting." She sniffed impatiently, catching the green wetness of the morning. Anyway, when Thad saw how things were working out just like she had said they would, he would have to admit it was the only way. He trotted toward her, the fringe of black hair bouncing on his forehead.

Marty counted the steps, waiting for him to speak, after he fell into place beside her. One, two, three, four. Longer than she expected. "What you gon' do with Ludie's pictures?"

"In case anybody wants to know, Thad Walcott," she said, her eyes on the town in the distance, "these are my drawings. I've spent every morning this week doing 'em in the woods."

That silenced him for six more steps, but his eyes

were burning holes in her cheek. "You lied to Mr. Ray? You're gonna be in a peck of trouble when everybody finds out!"

"Well, nobody's gonna find out unless you tell 'em, and you promised to God not to say anything," she snapped, turning to Thad, who was staring at the roll of pictures like it was a dagger dripping blood, for Christmas' sakes. "Besides, after your bigmama yakked like she did, causing Uncle Ray to make such a fuss about me going to Ludie's, it was all I could do."

Thad walked slowly, kicking up the dust and shaking his head sadly.

"Oh, don't be so grouchy. When people start buying the pictures, then I'll confess, like I told you yesterday. By then, nobody will care who drew them."

They were approaching the edge of town now, marked predominantly by Aaron Burr's jailhouse, a small, weathered shack of wormy wood, boarded and padlocked. A plaque to one side detailed the prominence of the structure as being the temporary detention site of the infamous American. Marty could never resist pressing her face against the splintery roughness for a look through the spaced boards, and she did so now. She had always imagined she might see Burr himself huddled on the dirt floor in chains. As had happened each time before, however, the only reward for her curiosity was the sight of the sunlight striping the dimness through the cracks.

"You're just gonna make things worse, keepin' on with it," nagged Thad behind her. "People down here don't like other whites pushing colored people on 'em, no matter how good they are at drawing or . . . or other things."

Marty wheeled around, her back against the shack. "How do you know so much? There's never been a colored like Ludie down here!"

Thad walked to an oak tree growing beside the jailhouse and sat on a root that humped over the ground. "Uh-huh. There was once. My father . . ." He stopped and began making circles in the dirt with his fingers.

"What about your father?" Marty leaned against the trunk of the tree. "What about him? You were going to tell me in the movies yesterday, weren't you? What about him, Thad?" Her voice was insistent.

"I shouldn't say. I promised Bigmama I never would, but well . . ." His shoulders heaved in a deep sigh. "Maybe it'll show you how things are. You promise never to say I told you about it?"

She owed him a promise, so she swallowed hard and nodded, feeling the closeness of conspiracy draw them together. "I do. I promise."

"Well, there was this colored man, Auntie Easter's son? And my father heard him sing. He was real good, as good of a singer as Ludie is an artist. My father was always bringing him over to Bigmama's to listen to him sing, and taking him places in the car, riding him in the front seat, and they spent an awful lot of time together, while Father was deciding how good a musician he was. He even was going to bring a man down from New York City to hear John—that was the colored man's name—but . . ." Thad stopped making circles in the dirt and brushed off his hands on his pants.

Marty thought she would die if he didn't hurry up and finish. "But what?" she asked, kneeling to look into his face.

He turned away. "Some people down here didn't like how my father was spending so much time with John. They started calling my father a nigger lover and things and were just about to come after him, and John, too, and beat 'em up." Thad's voice broke slightly, and he was silent so long that Marty wondered if he was going to continue at all. She looked to see if he was crying, but he wasn't.

"Well, did they? Beat 'em up?" There had to be more to the story.

"No. They didn't get to, because your aunt Letta came running over to Bigmama's and told my father, and he just left Caldwell and swore he'd never come back. He haddn't either, to this day. Nobody knows what happened to John. Bigmama said that Doodie told her they hanged him." Doodie worked for Miss Julia.

"For just being around your daddy? That's crazy!"

"Doodie said they made up another story about him

doing something bad to some white lady near Claxton, but everybody knew the real reason. He just got out of his place too much." He swung his eyes around to meet hers. "So that's why you got to forget all about making Ludie some famous person, before something happens to both of you!" His eyes were pleading.

"In the first place, I can't believe there are people all that mean in Caldwell, mean enough to do anything like that anyway, and in the second, if there is, why would your mama and daddy let you stay here?"

A giant ant was making its way up the rough tree bark, and Thad's eyes followed its journey. "My father wanted to take me away right then, Bigmama said, but Mother was traveling places with her music, so they decided I should just stay here until I was older and could make up my own mind about things. I pretty much have now, so I guess I'll leave next year when I start to high school." He turned back to Marty. "You ought to go on and tell Miss Letta and Mr. Ray the truth, right now!"

"I can't," said Marty, sticking her chin out stubbornly. "You said yourself nobody knows for sure what happened to that John, and even if he did get hanged, that was a long time ago." She moved away from the tree and began walking toward town again. "Besides . . ." she called over her shoulder.

Thad rushed around in front of her, walking backward. "Besides what?"

"Well, besides, somebody's got to do something for

people like Ludie and that John. That's all I know."

"Let grown-ups do it then. You can't make any real difference. You're just a girl. You'll only get yourself in trouble."

Her eyes were blazing when she looked at Thad. "You shouldn't of ever said that, 'bout me being just a girl. That's like spitting in my face, Thad Walcott. It's just going to make me do it all the more." She took a few steps, stopped, and shrugged. "It'll all come out all right. It has to."

"I wish I were going away today instead of next year," Thad said quietly. Then he turned and started home.

When Marty arrived at the store, she noticed that the Saturday-morning carnival was in full swing, and an assortment of dusty, faded trucks and other vehicles lined the road in front. That's good, she decided, more chance of selling Ludie's pictures. She saw Jewel leaning against the weathered post of his daddy's feed store, and she straightened her shoulders, smiling sweetly at him. Jewel didn't smile back. He looked sullen, mad even, as his eyes followed her to the door. When she had opened the screen, she peeked around it to see if he was still staring holes in her. He was.

As the congestion outside had indicated, Armstrong's General Store was, in Uncle Ray's words, "workin' alive" with customers. His sandy head bounced up and down behind the meat counter at the

rear of the store, and Marty was about to lay the
drawings on the counter and leave, since it looked as
if her uncle would be tied up for a while. Presently
he raised his head.

"Just a minute, little artist gal. I'll be right with
you," he said with a grin. To his customer, he added,
"Jack Dan, I want you to see some fine kind of drawings Martha's made. You and Ruth got to have one of
'em to put in your living room."

Marty winced. Her uncle's flattery embarrassed and
shamed her. She was anxious to leave. "I'll leave the
pictures on the counter, Uncle Ray. I promised Aunt
Letta I'd be right back with the mail."

"Go on, then, sugah," he said, coming from behind
the counter. "Tell Letta she best bring me up a dinner
plate too. I'll be too busy selling these Martha Armstrong originals to get home to eat." Chuckling, he
moved with Jack Dan Rountree to the pictures.

Outside the store Marty stood for a moment, glancing toward Turner's. Jewel was gone, at least. She
didn't know whether that made her glad or sad.

At the post office across the road she collected the
mail and started back down the broken sidewalk that
ran along the town road, toward home.

Next to the Pure Oil station a field of black-eyed
Susans added their goldenness to the hot haze of the
afternoon sun. Marty stood across the road gazing at
the mass of brilliance that this blend of nature had
created. It seemed out of place, somehow, next to the

grimy rustiness of the filling station, and she had an urge to capture the entire field, to move it to some other spot that might better suit its radiance.

She crossed the road, tucking the packet of mail under her arm, and waded in amid the yellow heat of the field. Soon her hands were sweaty as she plucked the tender threads, and heat waves puffed their raw greenness around her. If it weren't so hot, she thought, I would stay here, pick the field clean, and make a flower chain long enough to reach from here to Ludie. But the sun pushed fiercely at her and the letters grew damp under her arm, so after collecting twenty or so of the yellow-and-black weed flowers, she scuffed back across the road to the trees near the Burr jailhouse and sat on the root where, just a short time ago, Thad had pleaded with her to abandon Ludie.

The green juice of the flowers oozed under her thumbnail as she carefully slit each stem, weaving one flower into the next. The necklace complete, she slipped it over her head, and as she bent to get the mail, her heart lurched.

Something or someone was watching her from the jailhouse!

THIRTEEN

Marty rose slowly, her hands walking up the trunk of the tree. The road was deserted and quiet, save for the sounds coming from the filling station a half block away.

Despite the tingle of energy running through her, she could not make her feet move. In the distance the clank of a tire iron from Pure Oil gave her a start, and she began to edge toward the dilapidated jail-house. Her mind rambled crazily. How would Burr's ghost feel when she told him about cars and other modern things? What was George Washington really like? At the shack she pushed her forehead against the rough boards, finding a crack between them to peer inside. Exhaling slowly, she closed her eyes and opened them once more, to be sure. Empty as usual. It must have been her imagination. Aunt Letta was right, she guessed. Sometimes she did have too much for her own good. She felt giddy, and chilly, with relief, despite the warm air around her.

In the next instant fear again shot through her limbs like a lightning bolt! Hard, callused hands gripped her arms, shoving her against the old building. Throwing her head back, Marty saw the face of Jewel Turner above her. A frown hooded his smoldering eyes, and his mouth twisted in a sneer as he held her, pinned, against the jailhouse. When she tried to wrest free, his fingers dug deeper, and Marty could see dark parentheses of dirt under his fingernails.

"Jewel Turner! Let me go! What in the world's wrong with you?" she lashed out.

"Nothing's wrong with me! It's nigger lovers got somethin' wrong with 'em," he growled, jabbing her arms fiercely against the rough boards. She remembered Thad's story about his father, and the instant of rage she had felt at being abused faded into panic. When it finally came, her voice was thin and quivery.

"What are you talking about?"

He released her arms slowly, but did not move away, towering above her, his palms flat against the boards over her head. He wore no shirt with his overalls, and Marty was amazed to see hair under his arms as she stared up at him. Jewel's wild eyes raked over her.

"Hunh," he grunted, his face softening, to her relief. "I know one thing. That cute li'l ol' face ain't gon' be enough to keep you out of trouble down here, if it don't stay where it belongs."

Cautiously she eased out from under his arms, and to her surprise he stepped back, folding his arms against his chest. Marty stooped and picked up the mail she had dropped. "I still don't know what you're talking about, Jewel." Her courage was beginning to return.

"The hell you don't!" Marty caught her breath at the curse word. "What you don't know, Miss Martha Chafin Armstrong, is what color God made you, hanging around with niggers like you was one of 'em."

"I just went to see Ludie, Sister's girl, once, to make sure she wasn't a witch," she said with a toss of her head. "You better get your facts straight before you start picking on people!"

"Yeah," he answered sarcastically. "I know all about it, and facts say you been over yonder every day, and it wasn't Ludie you investigated neither. Chili ain't been in the fields for a week." Jewel's dark eyes searched her face in disgust. "Got yourself a nigger buck, ain't you, city gal?"

Why did everything come back to Chili? "What?" she yelled.

"Certain folks been watchin' you. We know what's been goin on. Know what to do about it too."

Marty could not believe it! First Uncle Ray and now Jewel believing she was mixed up with Chili. And they said she had too much imagination! She stepped boldly up to the boy.

"Listen here," she began, tapping the packet of mail against Jewel's arms. "Uncle Ray had the same crazy ideas you do, but he found out different. You just ask him what I was doing all this week. He'll straighten you out. Not that it's any of your business what I do anyway, but you just ask him, that's all." She was about to walk away when his hand reached out for her wrist, holding her fast.

"Mistah Ray ain't gon' say nothin' to get his little girl in trouble, but other of us, we know what's right." His other hand wrapped around her neck, pressing the velvet stickiness of the flower chain into her skin. "And we know how to handle this kind o' mess. We been doing it for a long time." Jewel released her wrist, pushing her forward roughly. "Just don't say you waddn't warned." He turned and walked away.

Marty stood, drained, watching the pull of Jewel's tanned back muscles in his side-to-side saunter toward town. Then she put her fingers to the place on her neck where his hand had pressed so cruelly moments before. Petals from the flowers there drifted over her shoulders. A stem broke, and the chain slid down to the red dust at her feet.

Maybe she should just forget about helping Ludie if things were going to get so mixed up. Maybe Thad was right. Thad. Suddenly an overwhelming sense of pity for her childhood playmate welled up. He had lived here all his life, feeling one way, acting another. That was probably why he stayed to himself so much. Why were people down here so mean anyway? The tears she had been holding began to drip down the front of her blouse, and stifling a sob, she turned and hurried toward home.

Her tears had dried, but there was still a lump between her ribs when she walked into the house. The Singer whirred from the rear of the house, and when Marty entered the dayroom, she found her aunt hunched over a machine, a pool of patterned chintz at her feet. When the machine stopped, Marty laid the mail at her aunt's elbow.

"Stars above, where you been, child?" Aunt Letta peered over her glasses. "Ray called. Said you left there thirty minutes ago. He wanted to let you know the good news." Before Marty could ask, her aunt rattled on. "Jack went and got Ruth, and she just fell in love with that raccoon picture. Said it looked just like the one Jack's hounds treed two years ago. But the best part is, you gon' get ten dollars for it!" She sat back and slapped her thighs with her hands. "Now! What you got to say about that?!"

The awful scene with Jewel vanished. All Marty could think about was that someone had actually paid cash money for one of Ludie's pictures. Ten whole dollars! It was just the beginning, too, she just knew!

"Oh, Aunt Letta. That's the best news in the world!" Marty clasped her hands under her chin and danced around the room. Now was the time, she thought. She pulled up a chair and sat next to her aunt at the sewing machine. "Now that the drawings are selling, Aunt Letta, there's something—" The jangle of the telephone interrupted Marty's confession.

"Sit right still—I'll be back, darlin'," her aunt said, rustling past Marty to get the phone in the hallway.

As she listened to her aunt's side of the conversation, Marty prayed her courage would last. She just had to tell Aunt Letta that the pictures were Ludie's, had to get rid of that guilty feeling, straighten it all out. When her aunt returned, however, with pride jumping from every pore, telling about still another sale, and how Gertrude Parker's son was going to make frames for the other pictures, and that Marty had better make her mind up to get busy and draw some more, well . . . Marty knew she couldn't dash everything to bits for her aunt. Not yet. She had to figure a better way, and more importantly, she had to talk to Ludie.

"I can't wait till your mama and daddy come back. They gonna have a big surprise waitin' on 'em, I'll tell you," said Letta, back at the machine.

"Yes'm, I know," replied Marty. Especially if I don't get a few things worked out soon. On her way out of the sewing room, she turned. "Did Uncle Ray tell you he might need a plate today?"

"Uh-huh," her aunt yelled over the noise of the machine. "I'm fixin' to take it, soon's I finish this seam."

Marty wandered out to the porch, sat on the railing, and swung her foot furiously. From Miss Julia's came the noise of the Hoover. Thad's mother was arriving later today, and Marty supposed the final touch-ups were under way. If only there were someone she could tell about Jewel's threats. Not Thad, certainly. He'd just say, "I told you so." At the sound of the horn in the driveway she looked up, watching her aunt back out of the drive and head up the lane toward town. When the car had turned onto the state highway, Marty started for Ludie's.

How happy Ludie would be when she told her about the pictures! Naturally she wouldn't tell her that everyone thought that she, Marty, had done them. Not yet. After all, it wasn't as if it was another lie. Still the same lie whether one person or another heard it.

High up in the pine trees of the woods ahead a crow cawed, then cawed again. Then another screech, and the yelp of a dog, came to her from the woods. Marty stopped at the edge of the trees, her breath coming in short jerks, from the heat and her brisk trot through the field.

Must be that dog's got something treed in the woods, with all that fuss he and the birds are making, she thought, passing beneath the first of the pine towers. She continued, following the trail of animal sounds, her curiosity growing. As she drew nearer, other noises—gruff, thumping, human noises—could be heard. She was almost in the heart of the forest now, her feet padding softly over the straw carpet as she raced toward the energy she felt from the sounds ahead.

Suddenly a wall of terror halted her, and she clapped a hand to her mouth to stop a scream that escaped anyway through her fingers. Chili lay face-down on the pine straw of the forest floor, his slinged arm pinned beneath him. The back of his woolly black head under Jewel's boot was smeared with blood, and his overalls had been ripped to the waist. Little Earl Cunningham and Grady Etheridge alternated stripes on the Negro's back with thick, evil straps of brown leather. The boy yelped, and Marty knew that it had been no dog that had brought her here.

She felt her eyes bulge. She couldn't stop staring at the scene of horror before her, as a sick fear spread through the tree of veins to her stomach.

"Get her!" It was Jewel.

By the time her brain had cut through her revulsion to tell her to run, a sweaty, hairy arm had pressed against her stomach, dragging her toward Chili. She opened her mouth to scream again and tasted salt from the hand over her face. Pinned against the smelly, hard flesh, she struggled, wrenching her head from side to side, trying to escape the smothering palm, but it only pushed harder against her nose, cutting off the air, and as the trees spun into blackness above her, she was almost certain she saw a scrap of blue cloth among them.

FOURTEEN

A rancid smell, like old oil, sifted through the gray mist covering her mind, pulling Marty to consciousness. Her eyes saw only soft darkness as she lifted her head slightly to discover her cheek pushed against the armrest of the backseat of a car.

A car that was moving, jostling her about, as its wheels fell into ruts and potholes of some rough road. The sudden appearance of a pair of heads, bobbing over the back of the seat ahead, triggered a nightmare of horror, and fear throbbed in her chest as she recalled Chili's bloody, striped back, naked and helpless against the awful straps.

Had they killed him? Where was he? She shifted, unpinning one leg from beneath her, and felt her foot touch something solid. Without moving her body, she slid her eyes to her foot. A small whimper seeped from her lips. Chili lay facedown on the floor of the car, his body, raw and bleeding, draped across the hump in the middle.

"She wake up?" Jewel's head swiveled, peering into the backseat.

"Yeah," replied Grady from the seat beside Marty. "Told y'all she waddn't dead. I didn't hurt her none."

"You liked to though. Then we woulda been in a mess!" Marty recognized the voice of Little Earl Cunningham. "Don't know why I let y'all talk me into this anyways. We get Bubba's car messed up with blood 'n all, he's gon' be mad enough to shoot me."

"Jes' too bad the little nigger lover come along when she did. We never woulda had to put 'em in here," Jewel declared. "Coulda gone off and left the nigger if she hadn't showed up."

"We shoulda left 'em both in the woods. I told y'all that's what we shoulda done; gawn on and left 'em there." Little Earl's voice sounded like some squawky musical instrument, sliding up and down the scale.

"Then she'd be blabbin' her mouth to everybody she saw, from Caldwell to Augusta," said Grady.

"So what, Grady?" said Earl. "Nobody'd care about a nigger gettin' beat up down here. Besides, it'd just be her word 'ginst ours."

Marty saw Jewel turn and stare out the window. "Nobody down here cares if we beat up a nigger, Earl, but she's somethin' different."

"Yeah, one o' them city gals," said Grady, leaning toward Marty. He had a strange gleam in his eye, and she watched in sick fascination while he ran a stubby finger down the length of her arm.

"Don't," she whispered, shrinking farther into her corner. How long had she been unconscious? Had her family missed her yet? She could see that it was still daylight at least. Where were they going? Warily, with one eye on Grady's hand, Marty eased herself upright.

"Best thing," continued Jewel, ignoring Grady, "is to keep 'em out of sight for a day or so, make it look like she run off with Chili, or he tak'n her some-wheres, till we decide how we gon' handle the whole thing."

"Ain't been a good nigger lynchin' in a long time," piped Grady.

It seemed an eternity while Marty waited for Jewel's comment. "Naw." Marty breathed a sigh of relief. "What about we get him to write a kidnap letter?" Jewel continued. "I think he can write, and we can get him to write a letter saying he's got her and Mistah Ray's gotta pay five hundred dollars to get her. Then . . ." Jewel's voice began to rise with excitement. "Then, we get the money and turn 'em loose. Every-body'll be on the nigger like a duck on a June bug, and it won't matter what Miss Citified says to anybody. Mistah Ray'll have the kidnap letter provin' the nigger done it!"

Marty was astonished. Did they really believe such a stupid plan would work? Suddenly she began to relax. Why should she be afraid of anybody that dumb?

"You know what?" Earl moved his head slightly toward Jewel. "By the time she gets back, starts tellin' her side, everybody's gon' think she's mixed up in the head anyways, being shut up with a nigger so long."

On the floor Chili stirred, moaning. With the toe of his boot Grady shoved the Negro's head down. "Shut up, coon."

Marty's heart pulled toward the dark figure at her feet, torn between her desire to comfort him and the fear of drawing more attention to herself.

"Where we gon' keep 'em though? That's what I want to know. I got to get Bubba's car back 'fore he gets home."

"I'll come up with somethin' 'bout that directly," said Jewel. "You just drive."

The car was silent for a while after that. Before long, Marty noticed that the tree shadows along the road were longer and the breeze blowing into the car had lost some of its heat. How long were they going to drive around the bumpy Georgia countryside anyway?

All at once Jewel spoke. "We'll put 'em back of Daddy's silo for now. That li'l ol' shed where he keeps tools 'n stuff. That'll do. Drive on out there, Earl.

It's far enough from the house, and nobody goes out there much this time o' year."

Marty stared forlornly out the window, not daring to speak, watching the familiar countryside slip by.

When the silo from Turner's came into view, Earl turned to Jewel. "Want me to turn down yonder?"

"Uh-uh. Go on down there till you come to that road 'longside of Cole Reid's place, then turn. That's the back way. It's longer, but it ain't as noticeable."

"Ain't nothin' but woods back there. We can't take Bubba's car through them woods, Jewel."

"Do like I tell you, Earl. There's a wide place through the timber where the log trucks go. Now go on."

Marty's head bumped against the glass of the window as the car dipped into the narrow rutted road she recognized as the way to Cole's. They didn't go long before turning again onto another path, the springs of the car squeaking over the weed-covered hollows. As tall brush swept the sides of the automobile, Marty heard Earl mumbling about the paint on his brother's car getting scratched. Obviously this route was not used by many people.

Marty felt her fear tighten another turn. She could be out here for days before they let her go. Suppose they did something awful to her, like they had to Chili? She could scream for all she was worth and nobody would hear. As the car jostled between the columns of pine trees, the hopelessness of her situation settled over her, and she put a hand over her mouth, choking back a moan.

"There it is. Right through yonder," Jewel said. "That there's the shed. Stop the car. Don't go all the way up to it. We can take 'em in from here."

The car stopped and the three boys got out. Earl came to Marty's door and opened it, letting in the pungent pine air. She glared at him, not moving. "Come on now, Martha Chafin. Get out, else I'll pull you out," said Earl, standing against the open car door.

"Never mind, Earl," said Jewel, coming around the front of the car. "I'll get her. You and Grady take care of the nigger."

"Huh," grunted Grady. "Might know Jewel'd get the good part."

Jewel reached into the car, pulling Marty's arm roughly as she shrank farther back against the seat. "This ain't what I'd call the good part," he said. "She's stubborn as a she-goat. Come on now, Martha."

"I'm not going in there," she said, her voice breaking.

Jewel's hands pushed between her back and the seat, digging into her spine. "Yes you are. Now come on, before I have to knock you in the head." He was tugging on her arms and back and suddenly, with a powerful jerk, pulled her from the car, throwing her against him with a thud. For a brief second he lost his balance, and as he righted himself his hands traveled, almost tenderly, Marty thought crazily, down the length of her arms, pressing her to him. She could feel his heart thump under his shirt, and his rusty boy smell sent strange stirrings, to battle with the anger and fear already at war within her. His voice was barely audible spoken against her hair. "You know I don't really want to hurt you, Martha, so just behave, hear?"

Out of the corner of her eye she saw Chili being dragged, Earl and Grady on either side holding him under his arms. Marty straightened and snapped free from Jewel's grasp. "I can walk. Just don't you touch me anymore, Jewel Turner."

Jewel's eyes were glazed with disgust. "Go on then, but don't try any funny stuff—I'm right behind you."

When she saw the shack, Marty decided she was about to find out how Aaron Burr must have felt, since the Turner structure resembled very closely the Burr jailhouse outside Caldwell: corrugated tin on the roof and rough, unpainted boards all around. She watched as Earl and Grady practically dumped Chili on the floor just inside; then she stepped in, her eyes squinting in the dim light. The air in the shack was damp and smelled like a mixture of wet croaker sacks and rusty metal. Indeed, in one corner there was a pile of old croaker sacks, and it was on here that Grady and Earl had tossed Chili.

"Y'all be careful with him. He's hurt bad enough

as it is." Marty hurried across the floor to kneel beside the Negro boy, carefully straightening his slinged arm, which had flung to one side.

"Look at her pawing that nigger," said Grady. "Mr. Ray would 'bout have a fit if he could see that."

"What my uncle Ray's gonna have a fit about is what y'all have done to us," Marty lashed out. "Can't y'all at least give me something to wipe off his face? It's all bloody and everything! Y'all hurt him bad!"

"Don't you know niggers don't feel pain the same as white people? That's why we had to whomp him so hard, to get through that thick black hide," Grady said with a smirk.

But Little Earl reached into his pocket and took out a kerchief. Marty snatched it from his extended hand. "Thank you," she said coldly. "Now get some water."

"What's she think this is?" Jewel asked. "Some kind of hospital? Ain't no water."

She looked from one to the other disgustedly, then put the kerchief close to her mouth and spit on it. Gently she began to wipe the dried blood from Chili's nose and mouth.

"White spit and nigger blood, mixed. Man, I seen it all now." Grady walked over and leaned against the side of the corncrib in another corner, eyeing Marty with disdain. "She sho' thinks a lot o' that nigger."

"Yes, I do," Marty said, getting to her feet. She went to Grady, her hands on her hips. "He's always been nice to me, which is more than I can say for y'all."

"Oh, we can be nice, too, Miss Martha." Grady sang her name, and with his rough hand he brushed her hair back, patting her cheek before she jerked away.

"Leave her alone, Grady. We got talking to do outside," said Jewel. "Y'all come on."

"Yeah, I got to get the car back," said Earl, starting for the door, followed by Jewel and Grady.

"Hey! Y'all can't just leave us here. It'll be dark soon and we don't have any water or anything." Marty pushed between Jewel and Grady.

"Get back, Martha. You think we're dumb enough to leave you here by yourself so's you can run off?" Jewel looked at Grady. "She must think we're stupid or something," he said, shoving Marty inside. "We got business to do out here. We'll be right back. Earl's gon' take Bubba's car home, and he'll bring some water 'n stuff when he comes back. Now, go on back in yonder with your nigger."

Marty stumbled across the floor and sat next to Chili on the croaker sacks as the door to the shack slammed shut. She drew her knees up and rested her head on them. At first there were just a few teardrops on her knees, but soon she was crying hard, not from fear or anger anymore. She cried because it seemed as though everything secure and sane in her world had vanished. She felt as if she could never count on anything or anyone again. She cried long and hard, as if she were desperate to cry, and when the tears slowed, she conjured up an image of her mother lying dead in her coffin and other sad things, to make the tears come again and keep coming until her soul was washed clean.

Presently she lifted her wet face, anger returning slowly, like an old friend. She'd show them. She'd make them pay good for what they had done to her and Chili. If it took the rest of her life! She could be just as mean as they could for what she thought was right!

And she was right—she knew it! Jewel, Earl, all of them down here, didn't consider the way they treated coloreds wrong, any more than they would stop to think twice about how they treated their livestock. Up until a week ago she might have shared their feeling. Had Ludie made such a difference in her thinking? Not really. Now that she was finally giving form to those spirits that had haunted her for so long, she was able to look back on any number of instances that had provoked unrest and discontent. The sight of a colored person standing on a bus on which there were vacant seats next to whites had often made her heart tighten. She could never see the logic to such conventions, but being a child, she had chosen the simpler course of acceptance.

No, her awareness of right and wrong began long

before Ludie, she guessed, although Ludie had made Marty realize that there were other forms of prejudice. She had done that all right. She smiled sadly, thinking of her friend. Ludie, whose intelligence, talent, and dignity broke through all her physical handicaps, whose warm, wise presence she longed for at this dismal moment.

A groan from Chili broke through her thoughts, and she laid a hand tenderly on his shoulder. She could feel the muscles move beneath her hand as he turned restlessly. "Chili?" Her face was at his ear as she spoke softly, in case he wasn't awake. "Can I do something?"

She saw the Negro boy's face screw up in pain and his lips move silently for a second before he answered. "Ain't no help, Miss." His breathing was labored as he struggled to speak. "Where we be?"

"I think it's some place back of Turner's, but I'm not sure. Oh, Chili, does it hurt awful?"

"Mostly wheah dey put mah overall strops back. Dey be rubbin' 'ginst de marks on mah back." He pushed himself up on one elbow. "Gots to git up. Do we gots watuh?"

"No, but Jewel said Earl was bringing some back."

"Wheah dey go?" Chili put his hand to his face, gingerly touching the welts.

Before Marty could reply, she heard the rustling outside that told her the boys were returning. The door rattled and Grady and Jewel stepped inside.

"Leave the door open, Grady, so we can see," said Jewel. "It's startin' to get dark." In the dimness Marty watched Jewel's face, hoping insanely that he had changed his mind and was about to let them go. But no, his features were still hard, as hate filled as ever. The boys came to stand above Marty and Chili, looking down on them like they were bugs.

"Well, this is what we gon' do," Jewel said.

"Yeah, y'all gon' git taught a good lesson." Grady chuckled and rammed his hands deep inside his pants pockets, rocking back and forth.

Marty glanced at Chili, the whites of his eyes luminous from the light filtering through the door of the shack. How many more lessons could they endure? She knew Chili was scared, too, but there was also a stubborn, fearless set to his jaw and chin.

"Boy," said Jewel, coming closer and kneeling down a short distance from his captives, "can you write?"

Chili nodded.

"Good, that'll be better," said Grady, doing a shuffle step and rubbing his palms against his thighs. "Be better if he did it, huh, Jewel?"

Jewel glanced at him hard, then turned back to Chili. "What you gon' do . . . niggah," he said, emphasizing the last word, "is to write us up a piece of paper telling how you tried to fool with Miss Martha here, but when she said she was gon' tell, you took her off somewheres, and since you knew you might end up hanging from a tree—"

"Yeah, yeah," sang Grady breathlessly. "Maybe that one right out yonder."

"Hush, Grady, let me get through." Jewel waved at the air between him and Grady as if swatting a mosquito. "Anyway, you realized you'd be in a heap o' trouble and you needed to get as far away from Caldwell as you could, and five hundred dollars would 'bout do it." He rested back on his haunches. "That's what you gon' write for us, and we'll see Mr. Ray gets it."

"We'll be yo' mail delivery, kind of," said Grady. "That's right. See how nice we are to niggers, Martha? Even deliver they mail."

Throughout Jewel's "fairy tale" Marty had been thinking that if it had been somebody in Caldwell other than her uncle Ray, their scheme might have worked. But not with him, no sir. Uncle Ray was too smart. He'd believe her word against these hoodlums any day. He wasn't like some other men in Caldwell, white men she had seen at church and in the store, who thought all women were good for was doing fluffy things. He'd pay attention to her when she told her side of things. She felt more confident now, and began to relax as she realized she wasn't in any immediate danger, that all they wanted was to get Chili in trouble. She couldn't wait to see their faces when she told Uncle Ray what had really happened. It was almost worth all of this.

"Well," said Jewel, getting up. "When Earl gets

back with the paper and pencil, you can start to writing. Hope he brings us something to eat too. I'm gettin' hungry, ain't you, Grady?"

"No suh," muttered Chili next to Marty.

"What you say, boy?" asked Grady.

"I say no suh," Chili repeated, and lowered his head, staring at his knees.

"No suh 'bout what? You ain't hungry? Good. You probably won't git nothin' nohow." Grady moved to follow Jewel to the door.

"I means no suh, I ain't writing no sech, what you said."

With a rush, Jewel swooped back down on one knee, catching at Chili's clothes and pulling the Negro forward.

"Let me tell you somethin', boy. You gon' write it. You gon' write as good as you can, too, 'cause if you don't, we gon' smash you and your fingers up so bad you ain't ever gon' write nothin', nuh pick cotton, nuh even pick your big black nose. You understand me? Do you?"

Marty watched with horror, waiting for Chili's answer. As Jewel pushed him back roughly against the croaker sacks, she could see pain on the boy's face. His eyes were watery and his upper lip glistened where his nose had begun to run. But Chili didn't speak again, just shook his head stubbornly.

"Let me talk some sense into him, Jewel." Grady

was coming toward them with a big shovel. "Me and this'll talk good."

Marty jumped up, coming between Chili and the two white boys. "Wait a minute. Y'all just go on." She looked from Grady to Jewel, pleading. "Please?" She still didn't know what she was going to do, but she had to say something to stop them from hurting Chili anymore. "I can—I can probably get him to write the note, but y'all got to promise me to leave him alone."

The boys stood silently. Jewel's brows came together as he considered what Marty had said. Grady's eyes, round and questioning, were on Jewel, and his hands clenched and unclenched the handle of the shovel. Several seconds passed while Marty held her breath; then finally Jewel nudged Grady with his elbow and turned to leave. "Come on, Grady. Put that down. You got more important business down at the Red Goose." Jewel chuckled low and ugly as he slapped Grady on the back. "Git on down yonder."

Her shoulders sagged with relief as Marty watched the two boys walk out the door. Her heart stopped when Jewel put his head inside again and seemed to fling his face at her. "Just remember. We ain't got all night for him to do it. Earl'll be back anytime now, and he better be ready to write. 'Nother thing. Don't be writin' it for him. It's got to be his hand." Marty continued to stare at the spot where his face had been, even after she heard the metallic scrape of the rusty latch.

She had no idea how to begin to convince Chili to do what they demanded, although Jewel's last remarks had sprouted the seed of an idea. She knew the hardest task before her was to convince Chili that everything would work out, if only he would trust her, that her uncle Ray would believe her when she told him how they had forced them to write the note.

"Uh-uh," Chili grunted, as if reading her mind. "Ain't gon' shame mah mama no sech a way. Dey jes' haft kill Chili fo' he write any sech."

"And just how do you think your mama would feel about that? Knowing her son was beaten to death like some . . . like some animal? Come to think of it, all you colored people get treated like dogs anyway. You may as well die like one!" She turned away, breathing hard. In the dim light she sensed Chili's eyes on her.

"Ain't how dey say it was."

Marty shook her head helplessly. "I know it, but I can't stand to see them do anything else awful to you, so will you please write it?"

"Ain't gon' write no lie."

She decided on another approach. "Chili, am I your friend or not?"

"You a nice girl, but I don't know 'bout bein' mah friend—you white."

Marty strained to see his face. "You're as bad as they are," she said with exasperation. "Friends are people you like to be with, no matter what color they are! You and Ludie are mine, whether you believe it or not. Now, will you, Chili, as my friend, write that thing, and trust me, as your friend, to make it right with Uncle Ray?" She didn't want to tell him what she had in mind until she had won his confidence.

Marty felt the energy of Chili's struggle beside her. A flock of geese high overhead was honking its way to a watery resting place, and she could hear Jewel and Grady murmuring outside. Finally Chili answered.

"Yes'm, Miss. I s'pose."

Marty wished he could see her smile. "You don't have to say yes ma'am, or call me miss either, Chili. You don't talk to your other friends like that, do you? Take my hand, friend Chili." She groped toward the spot where she thought his hand might be and presently found it. She felt him pull back at her touch, but she reached again and held the rough hand firmly in hers and began to shake it.

FIFTEEN

Now that fear for her personal safety had subsided, Marty found that being kidnapped was boring. It might have been better had there been light in the shed, but even talking to Chili was frustrating without being able to see his face. That pastime was out anyway now, since she could tell from his even breathing that he had drifted off to sleep again. Actually, being kidnapped reminded her of being sent to her room for punishment when she was small.

She started naming the state capitals, but that, too, was like punishment. For the life of her she could not see why they had someplace called Augusta as the capital of Maine, when the real Augusta was already in Georgia. Then there were Columbus, Georgia; and Columbus, Ohio, to make things even more confusing. And of course, Columbia, South Carolina. . . .

Without warning the door to the shed banged open against the wall. Jewel and Earl stood just inside, shining a big flashlight in her face.

"Here's you something to eat and drink," Jewel said gruffly, handing her a sack. "It don't matter to me what you do with it."

Marty opened the bag to find a jar of water, two cold biscuits, and two pieces of corn bread. She shook Chili awake and gave him a biscuit and the corn bread, then after taking a sip of water, passed the jar to him. The biscuit was dry and crumbly, not at all like Thelma's, and she would have liked to have had some more water, but she knew the boys were watching her and would probably have something to say about her drinking after Chili.

"What time is it?" she asked, swallowing a bit of the rough dough.

"It was nearly nine-thirty when I left the house," replied Earl. "I meant to wait till Mama and Daddy went to sleep, but Mama was up so long studyin' her Sunday school lesson, I fin'ly jes' told 'er I was gon' go on back down to the creek with Grady to git frogs." His breath came in jerks as he spoke and his fingers fumbled with the buttons on the front of his shirt.

"She don't want me stayin' out all night though, Jewel, like y'all said."

"We'll get him to write the note soon's he finishes eatin'," said Jewel. "After that comes the main part of this whole business, and you got to do it, Earl."

"What I got to do, Jewel?" Earl's eyes were large and he swallowed hard several times during the next few minutes while Jewel gave him his instructions.

"What you do is take the note and slip it underneath the latch of the screen door at Mr. Ray's store. He always makes sure he checks the store over real good, 'round 'bout midnight ever' Sat'dy, to be sure them niggers from the Goose ain't up to nothin' over there. He'll fin' it if you do like I tell you. Then you can go on back home. Grady'll be back with our refreshments pretty soon and me and him can watch 'em tonight."

Jewel put an odd kind of emphasis on the word "refreshments," and Marty was curious. She looked over at Chili, who was chewing slowly. From the way that his eyes shifted to the boys and back to the floor, she could tell he was still scared. At the mention of that word—"refreshments"—his eyes had widened and hung on a spot in the air in front of him.

"Well, I just want us to get on with it so I can get back home." Earl shifted from one foot to the other.

"All right, Earl. It don't matter. Give me the paper 'n stuff," Jewel growled. "I'll write down exactly what we want him to say."

From his shirt Earl withdrew a tan spiral notebook

and then fished in his pants pocket for a pencil.

Jewel took them and sat on the floor, looking thoughtful. He passed the flashlight to Earl and began to write. "Dear Mr. Armstrong," he began aloud. "Naw. Nigger wouldn't say that—he'd start right out with what he wanted."

"You gon' put in there 'bout him messin' with her 'fore he took her off?"

"Uh-uh. Mr. Ray's smart. He can figure that out hisself. Main thing is to say he got her and wants five hundred dollars before he turns her loose. Now hold that light up so I can see."

As she listened, Marty was struck again with how preposterous their plan was. Were they really that dense to think her uncle would believe any of this? All at once a cold stab of doubt pierced her confidence. Maybe she was the foolish one. After all, even though her uncle was not capable of doing what these boys had done to Chili, she knew that his ideas about coloreds were the same as theirs. She refused to let herself think it. Uncle Ray would believe her. He had to.

"Listen here." Jewel rose, reading from the paper in his hand. " 'Yore girl, Miss Martha Armstrong, is okay. If you want her to stay that way, put five hundred dollars in the mailbox in front of Miss Pansy March's house by five o'clock today. Signed, Chili Taylor.' " That was the first time Marty had heard Ludie's last name.

"That's what they said in a picture show I saw one time," Jewel said, giving the paper a snap with his finger.

"They said 'bout Miss Pansy's mailbox in the picture show?" asked Earl.

"No, Earl," said Jewel patiently. "Just the part about being okay and staying okay." He faced Chili. "Now, nigger, get ready to write." He started toward Chili, and the colored boy drew back, staring defiantly up at the white boy.

"Look. He'll . . . he'll write it," Marty spoke up quickly. "He told me he would, but . . . y'all just make us so nervous—"

She was interrupted by Grady's straw-colored head poking through the door. He carried two brown paper sacks with the necks twisted, outlining their contents. Marty realized then what the "refreshments" for him and Jewel were going to be.

"Hey, did he write it yet?" Grady wanted to know. "I got the stuff, Jewel. From the Goose, like you said. Whooee, we gon' have us some fun tonight!" He set the bags on the floor.

"Be quiet, Grady. Now, Martha," Jewel said, sarcasm heavy in his voice. "You sayin' somethin' 'bout us makin' y'all . . . 'nervous,' as you call it?"

"I really think it'd be better, quicker, if y'all went outside while Chili does it, that's all." If the plan she had formulated was to succeed, she and Chili must be alone.

Earl's and Grady's heads swiveled to Jewel, whose eyes darted from Marty to Chili.

"What difference does it make, Jewel, as long as the note gets written?" Marty said harshly.

With a growl Jewel handed the notebook, pencil, and draft of the note to Marty. "All right, but be sure he don't take all night." He turned to the other two boys. "Come on, y'all. All this thinkin' 'n stuff's made me thirsty as all get-out."

Marty breathed deeply as the door to the shed rattled shut behind them. Chili was staring at the note Jewel had written as though it were a rattlesnake.

"Don't worry, Chili. Here's what we can do," she said, moving closer to him. "First of all, does Uncle Ray know you can write?"

"He know I went to school, 'n he see me sign tickets fo' Mama at de sto'."

"Good, because he needs to know that you can write. See, the note's going to be in my handwriting, but signed by you, so right away he'll know something's fishy."

"Lak if you write, should be signed wif yo' own name."

"Exactly." She could hear the three boys outside laughing and gurgling. Marty didn't know much about alcohol, except that it was the "devil's drink," and she had no idea if you could get drunk from just one drink, but she decided she had better hurry and get the message written, just in case. It was extremely important for her to make contact with Uncle Ray.

Chili held the light, and she wrote swiftly, but not too carefully. Just enough to allow her uncle to recognize her writing.

She took the light from Chili, giving him the pad and pencil, and went to the door and looked out. The boys were sitting in a circle around a lantern, passing the devil's drink from one to another. She had to call Jewel's name twice before he looked up.

He rose and came toward her. Thank goodness he didn't walk drunk. "Did he write it?" he asked her. "Where is it?"

"He's just finishing," she replied, standing aside as Jewel brushed past her. He took the notebook, paper, and pencil from Chili and read what Marty had written. Her heart hammered, waiting for discovery. But it didn't come. He believed Chili had written it!

"You a good li'l nigger tender," he said, sauntering by her and brushing her cheek lightly with his fingertips. "Get on back in there now."

Marty was glad he hadn't taken the flashlight from her, and she settled herself down in the corner opposite Chili. Poor Chili. His lips were still puffy and blood was still caked at the corner of one eye, and all because of her.

"Chili," she said quietly after a moment, "I'm real sorry I got you into all this." The beam of the light danced over the walls as she spoke. "I only wanted to be friends with Ludie, and try to get her pictures sold, and I just made a mess out of everything."

"Ludie do draw good," he remarked, as though he had missed Marty's apology completely. "Been drawing like that since she was small, too, Mama say."

"Sister told me about the accident. I guess it was terrible for y'all."

"It be bad, dat's de truf. Mama say Mistah Ray and Miz Letta, dey was real sad about it, too, but won't none of dey doin's. Mistah Lonnie, he a wild boy back den—"

Her uncle's name wrapped around Marty's heart. Her shock must have shown on her face, because Chili stopped, his words frozen in midair.

"Miss Martha . . . M-Marty. You say Mama tol' you—"

"Not who the boy was!" she moaned. "Seems like my family's been causing trouble for yours for a long time, Chili." Could she ever see her uncle Lonnie again without thinking of Ludie?

All the boy-girl, growing-up speeches she had heard in the past week, not seeing Jun anymore, the terrified look on Aunt Letta's face when Chili's name was mentioned that day. Was it because they were afraid history might repeat itself, in the reverse? No wonder they had been so eager to embrace her lie about the pictures!

Somewhere a train whistled; a train filled with people, doing normal things like eating, reading newspapers, sleeping, while she was being kidnapped. How could this be happening to her and the whole world not know about it? Suddenly she felt weary, exhausted, and she curled herself around her knees.

At first she thought she was dreaming that Whipper, her cat, was pawing gently at her hair and the back of her neck. But Whipper couldn't speak, and with each caress her name was whispered in some distant, foggy place. She forced herself awake, and as she did so was aware of an awful odor, like decayed fruit. For a second or two she lay still, partly from curiosity—who was it?—partly from fear. Then as she felt the hand come around her waist and move slowly toward her breasts, she whirled herself around, upright.

"Grady!" she screamed. "You hog! You pig! You crud! Get away from me!"

In the corner Chili roused sleepily and shook his head, but before he could get up, Jewel had lunged from across the room, knocking Grady aside. Marty had not even been aware that Jewel was inside the shed, and now he lay across Grady, breathing hard.

"You want me to knock your head clean off, you just try something like that again." He looked over Grady's body at Marty. "Uh, what . . . Did he. . . ?"

"No, no, he didn't." She couldn't meet Jewel's eyes. "Just make him stay outside."

Jewel pulled Grady to his feet and pushed him toward the door. "Sleep it off ouchonder by the tree. You smell like a still."

Grady balked, peering down at Marty. "Whyn't you like white boys 'steada niggers, Marsa?" His speech was slurred. To Jewel he said, "Still dark, lannernsout."

"Give him the flashlight," Marty said disgustedly.

Still grumbling and carrying the light, Grady went out. Jewel followed and presently returned with the lantern and lit it, placing it next to him at the far side of the cabin. He stretched his long legs and sat with his back against the wall. In the dim glow from the lantern Marty could make out the hard set of his jaw, and the eyes, staring sadly, she thought, into space.

"I'm sorry about him. I didn't mean for nothing like that to happen."

"It's no worse than what y'all did to Chili," Marty said.

"That's some of it. Boys don't have no respect for white girls that take up with niggers. Ain't never heard of no decent girl acting like you do. I thought you was different." Jewel's voice held an edge of expectancy, as if he hoped she had some explanation.

She shrugged. Maybe if she were older, she could find the right words to make him understand, but not now, not in this situation.

The windowpanes above Jewel's head had gone from black to gray, tinged with gold. She had never seen dawn; even when they went to sunrise services at Easter, it was already light out. She wondered if she would actually be able to see the sun slide up, the way it showed in pictures.

Jewel craned his neck, looking over his shoulder through the window. "Soon be morning."

"Then what?" Her eyes roamed his face, searching hopefully for some sign of relenting. She knew better. Things had gone too far now.

It was depressing to think of staying in the smelly shed another whole day, until five o'clock, when . . . *if* . . . Uncle Ray gave them the money. Up until that moment the possibility that he might not had never occurred to her. Suppose her uncle didn't have five hundred dollars? Her empty stomach pulled on this new concern, making her queasy.

"You gettin' sick?" asked Jewel, his dark eyes narrowing. "You look funny."

"How'd you look if it was you being kidnapped? Besides, all I've had to eat since yesterday is that ol' dried-up biscuit."

Jewel stood up and looked out the window. "I reckon I could try to sneak in the house 'fore anybody's up and get us something." He walked to the door and opened it. "Grady's dead to the world, so he won't bother you, but I'll lock you in, just in case."

After he had closed the door and locked it from the outside, he said, "It won't do you no good to make a racket either. Only one to hear'll be Grady."

She listened until the sound of his footsteps had died away, then curled her knees up, pulling one of the sacks around her. The air was damp and chilly, and she tucked her elbows in to warm her arms.

Her thoughts turned to her family. They must have found the message by now. Marty's heart hurt at the picture of fluffy little Aunt Letta, wringing her hands in despair, her gray eyes, all round, looking to Uncle Ray for comfort. He'd be worried, too, she was certain, but mostly . . . well mostly, Uncle Ray would be as mad as a "wet settin' hen," she thought, using her aunt Letta's expression.

A faint tapping noise on the window disconnected her imagination. The sound came again. It better not be Grady, she thought with alarm.

In the corner Chili stirred, propping himself up on his good arm to stare at the window.

"Stay there," she told him, making her way cautiously across the shed. At first, looking straight ahead, she saw nothing, but then, pressing her head against the window and peeking sideways, she was nearly overcome with happiness at the sight of Jun and Ludie, crouched at the back of the shed. They saw her and edged to the window. Marty tugged and tugged, but the window, unopened for many years, wouldn't budge. She was so afraid Grady would wake up or Jewel would get back!

"Grady?" she said softly, through the pane.

Ludie inclined her head on folded hands to indicate

that Grady was still asleep. "Jewel will be back soon," Marty told them.

By now Chili was at her side. "Git dat sack and holt it 'ginst de pane," Jun told Chili.

After several minutes and a muffled crunch or two the dusty panes were out, and seconds later the rotting wood of the frame snapped, to provide a sizeable opening. Although the window was low to the floor, Marty was not tall enough to step over to freedom, so Chili lifted her up and out into Jun's arms. Then she stood outside, next to Ludie, and watched as Chili made his way through. Ludie smiled and patted Marty's shoulder. So many questions, but Marty knew she would have to wait for answers.

Jun nodded his head toward the woods, and the four of them trotted softly away, leaving the night and its memories.

Within an hour Marty was sitting at the oilcloth-covered table of Cole's wife, Ruth, eating fried fat-back, biscuits, and egg gravy. She still couldn't get the grits down.

When they had arrived at Cole's, it had been "Git on in heah," "Musta been scairt to def," and "Sot yo'self down to breakfas'," and Marty had not had the chance to question Ludie and Jun about the details of their rescue. When they had relaxed, she learned that the flash of blue she thought she had seen before she lost consciousness in the woods had been Ludie. The Negro girl had watched as the white boys stuffed

Chili and Marty into the car and pulled away, then she had run home to tell Sister. Their first thought had been to go to Mr. Ray for help, but they had decided against that.

Years ago, at the time of Ludie's accident, it had been the Negro who had been blamed for "enticing" the white boy in the first place. Sister decided they might do Chili more harm than good by bringing whites into it, and that they could best handle the rescue themselves. Later Ludie had gone into town to see what she could learn.

As Jun, who was telling the story, explained, "Mos' whites b'lieve Ludie tetched, cain't hear good neither." (The same as I did, thought Marty.) "So Ludie, she go to Turner sto', thinkin' to hear somethin' won't be said roun' reg'lar folks."

The only thing Ludie had learned, said Jun, had been that Jewel was supposedly at Lake Sinclair, fishing, for the weekend. On her way back home Ludie had met Jun, who was coming to the Red Goose, where he worked on Saturday nights. She had shown him the description of the incident she had written for Sister, and he had told her he had seen the car turn down the lane toward Turner's property when he started out that afternoon. The rest was easy, since Jun knew all about the shed. Marty was amazed to learn that Ludie and Jun had kept watch over them all night from the woods near the shed, and that they had nearly intervened when Grady frightened Marty.

"Well, now," said Ruth. "Speck this chile need to git on. Cole say he see dem boys come scootin' out yonder 'while back." To Chili she said, "You stay on and git dem places on yo' back fixed."

Marty had not given a thought to what Jewel and Grady would do when they found she and Chili were missing. Now, climbing into the truck next to Cole and Ludie, she began to worry that they might run into them on the ride home. When they passed the reedy path leading to the shed, Marty tried to make herself small.

"Don' bother yo'self, Miss. Dem boys long gone," said Cole.

Ludie laid a comforting hand on Marty's leg and smiled her lopsided smile, though Marty thought she detected a hint of concern in her eyes.

Soon they were on the state road again, and the ride became smoother. The sun was well up and shining brightly, and Marty's heart began to race as they neared her uncle's house. She was glad Chili wasn't along. It would be difficult enough to convince them that Chili was as much a victim as she was, and if he were there, Marty was sure, everyone would just jump all over him right away, never hearing her side of the story.

They were nearing the turnoff to the house, and Marty glanced toward Sister's. No smoke today. Sunday. A piece of gravel pinged the side of the old truck as it turned down the long lane. What she saw ahead caused Marty to suck in her breath sharply. A dozen cars surrounded her uncle's house, but Marty saw only one: the blue-and-white Ford that had brought her to Caldwell a week ago, her parents' car. She pointed to it, looking at Ludie, but the Negro girl was looking across the top of Marty's head at Cole.

All at once the impact of what she had set in motion, and the lives touched by it, combined with the fear and exhaustion from the night before, poured in on her. Ludie, sensing her struggle, drew Marty close, and within seconds the colored girl's shoulder was damp with Marty's tears.

SIXTEEN

When Cole's truck stopped in the driveway, the screen door banged open and Beth Armstrong bounded down the porch steps, her arms outstretched.

"My darlin' angel! Thank the good Lord you're safe." Her mother's eyes seemed even bluer against her tanned skin, and Marty noticed she was wearing a dress she had not seen.

As Marty stepped from the running board of the truck, she saw Uncle Ray, her father, and Aunt Letta come from the house. For several moments she stood in the driveway, pushed, pulled, patted, and held by her family.

"Precious Martha," her mother whispered against her hair. "Was it just awful?"

"Yes'm," said Marty aloud. "You should have seen what they did to—"

"Let's don't talk about it out here," Beth Armstrong said quickly, placing an arm around her daughter. "Come on inside, everybody."

Marty glanced over her shoulder at Ludie standing nearby.

"Ludie can stay out here if you want her to, darlin'," said Aunt Letta.

Ludie nodded, meeting Marty's eyes over her aunt's head.

"But—" Marty started to protest, then allowed herself to be brought into the house and "comforted."

Inside it seemed just the way it had at her grandfather's funeral. Neighbors and friends sat around on straight chairs; the dining room table was loaded with food. The people seemed faintly disappointed at Marty's appearance. Like the party was all over and they had no place else to go. Marty recognized Gertrude Parker; Jewel's mother, Maybelle; Miss Julia; and others she had seen and known in Caldwell most of her life.

"Excuse me, y'all," said her aunt, making her way through the livingroom, Marty and her mother in tow. "We got to get some nourishment into this child."

Marty nearly said that she had eaten already at Cole's, but thought better of it.

Thelma moved a pound cake to one side on the kitchen table and Marty sat down, toying with the plate of food her mother had given her. Why did everybody think food was a cure-all? She sighed and sat back in the chair. Thelma had not spoken a single word to her, but stood now, her huge hands hanging like hams at her side, staring at Marty.

"Thelma," she said tiredly, "I'm fine, really. They didn't hurt me."

"Who do it?" Thelma's great head shook slowly, back and forth. "Won't Chili lak dey say, wuh it?"

"Oh, my gosh! Chili!" It was the first time since walking in the front door that Marty had even thought about sorting things out. "Chili didn't do anything but get beaten up within an inch of his life!"

"Ain't what dey sayin' ouchonder. De menfolk outside now settin' up to git 'im."

"No!" Marty pushed back the chair and started for the back door. The sharp tone of her voice brought her mother and aunt to the kitchen.

"Martha Chafin," her mother said, catching her arm. "Come on back in here and quiet down. Your daddy and Uncle Ray can take care of everything!"

"No, Mama!" she cried, wrenching free. "They're wrong! I've got to tell them how it was!"

"Martha, now you come on back here. . . ." Her mother's voice trailed behind her as Marty rounded the side of the house to the driveway.

Her father, Mr. Narvel Turner, Uncle Ray, and

some other men were standing beneath a cloud of cigarette smoke, next to a car she didn't recognize.

All eyes turned in her direction as she hurried toward the group, frantically calling her uncle's name. Her father reached out for her, holding her fast against him.

"It's all right, Martha," he said. "We'll take care of everything now. Go on back in the house with the ladies."

"Not until you listen to me! All of you!" she shot back angrily. Jerking from her father's grip, she moved to one side, a few yards from the men. "Y'all may think I'm only a silly girl, but I know what went on yesterday better than anybody out here, 'cause I was there. Chili Taylor didn't have anything to do with any of it!"

"What about this here piece of paper?" Narvel Turner fluttered the note Marty recognized so well.

"I wrote that!" she said, looking at her uncle in disbelief. "Didn't you recognize my writing, Uncle Ray? I thought surely that would tell you something. Jewel and them wanted Chili to write it, but I knew if the note was in my handwriting, you'd—"

"Back up, young'un." It was Mr. Turner. "What you talkin' 'bout, Jewel?"

"But . . ." She looked from one to another. "That's who took me away and beat up Chili!"

Mr. Turner shook his head from side to side, chuckling. "Li'l gal, Jewel's been up to Lake Sinclair

all weekend. He ain't been nowhere near here."
Everybody else must have thought it was funny, too,
because shortly there was a round of laughter. Marty
felt her face get hot.

"I'm sorry, but you're wrong, Mr. Turner. Jewel
was in that shed at the edge of your property last night
keeping Chili and me locked up. He and Little Earl,
and Grady Etheridge too."

"Martha Chafin! You know better than to dispute
an adult's word!" Her father was staring at her as if
he didn't know who she was.

"I can't help it, Daddy. I can't let them do anything
more to Chili!"

His neighbors looked at Ray Armstrong, asking with
their eyes that he settle his niece so they could go
about their business. Finally he turned to Marty, his
face grave, speaking quietly in contrast to her last
outburst.

"All right, Martha. Come on over here and tell us
your side of things," he said, his black eyes weary.
"But be sure you get it right." Special emphasis on
the last word.

The men by the car parted, their faces tight, as
Marty walked through their midst to stand against
the front fender. Her heartbeat rang in her ears and
her mouth tasted silvery, like tinfoil. So much de-
pended upon what she said now, perhaps Chili's very
life!

Quietly and a little breathless at times, Marty told the story of her journey into the woods yesterday, of Chili's beating, her fainting, the drive to the shed and the night that followed. She was careful not to color the incident with her own recently adopted racial philosophies, but kept strictly to the facts. From time to time the men would murmur among themselves, and she knew they were having doubts. Although she avoided the eyes of her father, who looked at her as though she were a puppy who had piddled on the rug in front of company, she could not resist the face of her uncle, and watched it change from tolerant sympathy to hard defiance as her story unfolded. Of all people, he was the one she wanted most to believe her.

When she had finished, she searched the faces around her for some sign of acceptance but saw only heads shaking in disbelief.

Uncle Ray came slowly toward her, his eyes soft again. "Martha honey, one of the reasons that you're so appealin' is 'cause you're such a bright child. 'Course, part of that comes from an active imagination." Martha dropped her eyes, defeated. He hadn't believed her at all. She didn't speak, but let him finish.

"Imagination is a fine thing to have, but every now and again, when you put it on top of strain, and all of us know you been under a bad strain, well, it's just possible that what actually occurred last night is way down on the bottom of your mind, covered up with what you thought went on."

"But you saw the note, Uncle Ray? My writing! Doesn't that tell you anything?"

"Tells me you were somewhere with Chili."

"That's right." Mr. Etheridge, Grady's father stepped forward. "But why you have to go smirchin' my boy's name saying them things, 'bout him drinking whiskey and takin' you off somewheres?"

"Jewel, too, when he waddn't nowhere around!" said Narvel.

Marty looked from one to the other, feeling like a trapped animal, as the murmurs from the men began again. They began to disperse, and started down the driveway toward the cars. As her uncle followed after them, Marty ran up to him.

"Uncle Ray, please don't let them hurt Chili! I didn't make it up! I'll swear on the Bible!" She was fighting terribly hard to hold back the tears as her hands gripped her uncle's arm.

He turned to his brother, still standing in the yard. "George, come get her," he said, gently prying loose Marty's fingers from his arm.

As she swung her head from her father back to her uncle, Marty caught sight of Ludie, sitting on the side of the front porch, and she cried out.

"Wait! All of you! Ludie can tell you! She was there in the woods. She'll show you!" Marty ran to her friend. "Write it for them, Ludie," she begged. Behind her she could hear men snickering.

Ludie looked at Marty in hopeless confusion, then at the men, who had begun walking again.

"They're going after Chili! Please, Ludie! You have to show them! You have to try and make them believe!"

"Martha Chafin," her father called. "Leave that poor creature alone!"

Something seemed to flare up in Ludie's eyes for just a second, then she put her hand into her pocket and withdrew her pad. From the corner of her eye Marty saw her aunt come to stand over Ludie on the porch. The colored girl marked on the pad for several minutes. Precious minutes, thought Marty, afraid they might lose the attention of the group. All at once she heard Aunt Letta gasp. Her aunt's eyes were glued to the paper in Ludie's lap.

"Ray," she called to her husband, "come here and look at this, would you?"

Marty stood beside her uncle and gazed with him at the pad. Ludie had not written, but sketched, the entire incident in the woods. The features of the figures were fuzzy, drawn in haste, but the sketch left no doubt that there were four males and one girl.

"Don't prove nothin' to me," one of the men said, over Uncle Ray's shoulder.

"It proves something to me," Marty's uncle said, so softly she could barely hear him.

He knows about the pictures now, she thought as her eyes locked onto those of her uncle. Now he was sure to think she was lying about everything!

"May I see what is on the paper?" The voice was husky and its tones round and full. Marty looked at the corner of the porch to see a tall, dark-haired lady approach. She had not seen Thad's mother in years but instantly remembered the large emerald eyes, so identical to those of her son.

Naomi Walcott scanned the picture Ludie had drawn, then returned it to the girl. Their eyes touched gently in some ancient recognition, and Naomi smiled. "Well, Ludie, you're quite an artist!" Turning to Ray Armstrong, who had begun walking again toward the cars in the driveway, she called, "Ray, I know this is none of my affair, but—"

"You're right about that, Naomi," he returned over his shoulder. "You don't know about anything down here anymore."

"Oh, but I do," she countered, coming to stand amid the group of men. "And I guess that's why I don't live here any longer." She made an impressive figure, nearly a head taller than some of the men. Even in her faded slacks and baggy shirt, Marty thought Naomi looked like a queen addressing her subjects. "Listen to me, please," she continued. "Then, if you want to go tracking that boy, you can. But first, will you just hear me out?" Not one man moved. It was as though they were bound by Naomi's commanding presence, held on some invisible leash. "For the moment put aside your apparent hunger for a good 'nigger stomp' and think. Forgetting what Martha has told you, Ray." Naomi hesitated, her green eyes burning into those of Marty's uncle. "You owe Sister's family." She smiled wryly and shrugged. "Well, much, but in this instance you owe them the benefit of the doubt, at least. First of all, assuming that Ludie and Martha may be telling the truth—" More mutterings, and Naomi held up her hand to still them. "Assuming, I said. What would the good citizens of Caldwell do anyway to three white boys who had beaten up a Negro and abducted a white girl who they felt had had a friendship with him?" She looked around the group. "Nothing. Absolutely nothing, because these boys would have been acting as is customary in Caldwell, where it is custom, not law, that dictates how people behave toward one another. Nothing, because it is not customary to punish whites for abusing coloreds. So, all of this considered, what do you have to lose by bringing the accused and their accuser together?" She turned to face Letta Armstrong on the porch. "At the least, you might find out your niece is no liar!"

"Naomi's right, Ray," said Beth Armstrong, coming down the steps. "I, for one, would like to know if my daughter's telling the truth. Can't one of y'all go get those boys, to see how they act in front of Marty?"

"This is the biggest pile o' hogwash I ever heard in

my life," said Narvel Turner. "Standing out here like dumb animals listening to some Yankee nigger lover tell us how to act. I wouldn't bring my boy down here even if he was home, which he ain't." He stepped to the edge of the porch and called inside to his wife. "Maybelle, get in the car. We goin' home." To Uncle Ray he said, "If y'all decide to go after the nigger, let me know."

"Ray," Marty heard her aunt call, "what about the others?"

Uncle Ray turned to Mr. Etheridge. "What about it, Lewis? You willin' to go get Grady?"

"Shoot, yeah, Ray. Ain't gon' make a particle of difference, though. I'll even pick up Little Earl, if it's all right with Carl," he added.

"I'll go with you," said Little Earl's daddy. "Anything to get this mess over with."

When the Cunninghams and Etheridges had gone, the remaining families began straggling from the house, and very soon only Armstrongs and Walcotts remained. And Ludie.

The whole time his mother had been speaking to the group, Thad had remained behind, halfway between the Armstrong house and Miss Julia's. Now he inched slowly forward, his eyes on Marty. She could feel them, and she wasn't about to face Thad yet. Deliberately she went up on the porch and sat in the rocker behind Naomi and Ludie, who sat on the side of the porch. Thad walked to the pillars at the side of the steps and sat down.

"Thad, sugah, they's some of Miss Maybelle's pecan pie in yonder, if you want it. Thelma'll get it for you." Aunt Letta had not given up her role as hostess.

Ugh, thought Marty. Pecan pie at nine o'clock in the morning, for Christmas' sakes.

Thad shook his head, declining Aunt Letta's offer, and cut his eyes toward Marty again. She turned away, listening to Naomi and Ludie. Well, listening to Naomi, watching Ludie respond with her pad and pencil. Marty wanted so badly to tell Thad's mother about the pictures at the store, but thought it best to clear up the matter at hand before going into Ludie and the pictures. Her mother was telling her aunt all about their week at the resort, and from the driveway came the voices of her uncle and father discussing the crops. All these people having perfectly normal conversations, apparently unaware of the reason that had brought them together. She wanted to shout at them, make them bring their talk back around to what should have been uppermost in their minds. She wanted Naomi to tell her something, anything, that might make everyone believe her instead of Grady and Earl. She knew she was smarter than the boys, and if necessary she could probably outtalk them, but then there were the grown-ups and their strange kind of justice where coloreds were concerned.

With each car that whined by on the state road, her heart jumped. Two squirrels chased each other up and around the trunk of the pecan tree, and from Miss Julia's magnolia a jay squawked. What was taking them so long? She was anxious to confront Grady and Earl, but when she imagined the scene, herself and Ludie . . . No, she couldn't count on Ludie, for in spite of what they had seen moments before, she knew the men would never accept Ludie's account. It would be her word against that of Grady and Earl. Her mind was in lonely turmoil as it searched for some ally who might stand beside her, who might be believed. Like gears moving in her head, her thinking suddenly shifted. How dumb I am! Mama, Daddy, Uncle Ray, and Aunt Letta are my family. They want to believe me, I know they do. I know they do. But there was still that knot in her stomach.

Suddenly they were there.

Mr. Cunningham and Mr. Etheridge got out first, from the front of the car, and it seemed an eternity went by before the back door opened and Grady and Little Earl stood in the driveway. They looked just the same, even wore the same clothes. Little Earl stared at the ground, and Grady looked up at the tops of the trees in the yard, his hands in his pockets.

Anger and anxiety chased each other in Marty's head, like the squirrels she had watched moments before. When she looked at Grady, all she could think about was the feel of his putrid hands on her skin the night before, and she sprang quickly from her chair, dashing to the porch steps, ready to rush forward with her accusations. Something stopped her, and she took a deep breath before proceeding slowly down the steps and across the yard to face the two boys.

Their eyes had gotten big and wary as they watched Marty walk calmly toward them, but when she stood, finally, in front of them, Grady and Earl looked away.

"Grady, Earl," she said, her voice quivering. She would have to be stronger, she told herself. "I just want y'all to know I forgive y'all for what y'all did." Thank goodness, her voice was steady now. "There's just one thing. I don't think anything else should happen to Chili. These men want to find him 'cause they think he was the one that kidnapped me. But you know, and I know, that it wasn't Chili at all, so just tell the truth and nothing'll happen to you."

"What's she talkin' about, Earl?" Grady mumbled. "Do you know?"

"Uh-uh, I don't know," Earl said, with a faint sniff.

Sensing Earl as the weak spot, Marty pushed on. "Yes you do, Earl. Remember, you had Bubba's car and were all worried about getting Chili's blood all over inside?"

From the corner of her eye she saw Mr. Cunningham look sharply at his son.

"And then," Marty continued, "when we went through those tall weeds on the way to the woods, how worried you were about the fenders getting scratched?" She stood closer to Earl now, bending down to peer up into his downcast face. "You know I'm telling the truth, don't you, Earl?"

"Get away from him," Grady said, edging himself between Marty and Earl. "You just makin' up stuff!"

"No, I'm not, Grady, and you know it!" Turning to Mr. Etheridge she said, "Why don't you ask Clay Williams at the Red Goose if he sold Grady liquor last night, Mr. Etheridge?"

"Just be another nigger lie, if he said he did," said Grady.

"Okay, then. Mr. Etheridge, do you know for sure where Grady was all night?" Marty took a step forward, in the direction of Grady's father.

"Uh, sure do. He was campin' out all night with Little Earl, up by the creek. They was gon' fish, or gig frogs or something or other." Mr. Etheridge looked at his son for confirmation of what he had said.

Marty heard Mr. Cunningham, Earl's father, clear his throat, then saw him turn to Mr. Etheridge. "Well, Lewis. Hold on jes' a minute. Little Earl did go out earlier last night, but he come home well 'fore midnight. I heard him ride in on his scooter."

"That's right, Mr. Cunningham!" Marty was excited. Things might work out after all. "Little Earl came to the shed on his scooter about nine-thirty or so, to bring us some food and water. I remember because I asked what time it was and Earl said he would have been back sooner, but he was waiting for Mrs. Cunningham to quit studying her Sunday school lesson and go to bed, but she never did so he told her he was going to the creek. Then he said he would have to go on home after the note was written. You must have heard him come in right after he dropped the note off at Uncle Ray's store."

Grady and Earl locked eyes, each looking desperately at the other for a way out.

Finally Earl tore his eyes from Grady's and whirled at Marty. "You're lyin'! We didn't get no blood on Bubba's car, or scratches, or do anything like what you said! You're lyin' is all. Bubba's car is fine, and I was at home!" He faced Grady, panting. It was every man for himself.

"Yeah, Daddy," Grady said to his father. "Uh . . . uh . . . See, I went to . . . Me and Earl went to the pond, but then Earl said he couldn't stay, so after he left, I just went on and fished by myself, then fell asleep." He turned to glare at Marty. "This here girl's lyin' through her teeth, 'bout everything!"

Marty marched forward, pushing her face close to Grady's. "Well, Grady, I did lie about one thing, I admit it."

"See?" he said, turning to Earl in triumph.

"I lied," Marty continued, "when I told you Chili wrote the ransom note. I wrote the note for him to let Uncle Ray know that Chili wasn't responsible for my being gone." She forced a soft laugh. "But you and Jewel were so dumb, you believed he wrote it all the time!"

"Naw, we didn't!" Grady snarled. "You didn't fool us for one li'l biddy minute. Soon as Jewel saw it, he knew you wrote it, but he said it didn't really matter, that we'd—" The boy stopped, aware of what he'd just admitted, conscious of all eyes on him.

Marty's shoulders drooped as a great gust of air left her. She turned to see her uncle beside her.

"This means, then, boys, that Martha's been telling us the truth? 'Bout it all?"

Silence hung in the air beneath the trees. Even the squirrels had stopped chattering. Then, from the distance, came the peal of the church bells. It was Sunday, after all. Marty heard a snuffle and looked at Earl, who was wiping his nose.

"Boys?" repeated Uncle Ray. "Little Earl? Y'all aren't gon' get hurt. Just tell the truth."

Little Earl rubbed the palms of his hands down the side of his pants and nodded. "Mr. Ray, we didn't go to hurt nobody but the nigger, honest. Jewel thought we ought to scare him to stay away from white girls, like, but then . . ." He glanced nervously at Grady, who looked at him with disgust. "Well, we never would've carried her off if she hadn't come through the woods when she did 'n all. It's jes'—"

"All right," said Ray Armstrong. "Y'all go on. We'll get everything straightened out directly."

The boys' fathers made a small show of scolding them as they herded them back into the car. When they were gone, Uncle Ray said to Ludie, "Tell Chili I'm gon' want to see him, too, after 'while."

Alarm showed briefly on Ludie's face. "Yanh?"

"Nothing bad, Ludie. I just want to talk to him."

"Yanh, yanh." The blue kerchief jerked quickly up and down before turning, with its owner, and bobbing down the lane toward the state road.

As she watched her friend, Marty felt a tremendous sadness well up within her. She couldn't let Ludie just hobble away without even thanking her for all she had done! She had to talk to her, tell her about the pictures, other things too! "Ludie, wait," she called, trotting across the yard after her friend.

"Martha," her mother's voice rang behind her. "I want you to go in the house and lie down. Right now!"

"But, Mama." She turned, her voice insistent. "I need to see Ludie. Really I do. Please?"

Ludie had stopped and stood in the lane facing Marty, her strange features working toward a smile. "Yanh, yanh." She nodded, motioning Marty back toward her family.

Marty stayed, watching her friend make her way down the lane, her crippled foot leaving a trail in the red dust. "Maybe tomorrow," she said, so softly she didn't think anyone had heard. Behind her she heard husky laughter and looked back into Naomi's face.

The lovely green eyes were bright, as Naomi

brushed a hand over Marty's hair. "Young lady, I have a feeling that you and Ludie will share a good many tomorrows." Then, patting Marty's back, she pushed her toward the house. "Now, get on in the house like your mother said."

SEVENTEEN

Hands stroked her face, her arms. Rough, scratchy hands, running over her skin, caressing her, squeezing her gently. Up her back, playing with her hair, moving it back to let in hot, damp breath, rotten-apple breath, on her neck. Grady's breath, Grady's face, Grady's hands.

No! She pushed him away, her hands against the hard bone and soft skin of his face. Still he pawed and groped at her, pushing her down, rubbing his face over her chest. Frantically she tossed from side to side, trying to shake him off, but he only moved with her; grunting, moaning, animal moves. She couldn't get away from him. She had to get away; had to see about the tapping on the window. Her breath came hard, she was so frightened, and Grady was so heavy. How could she get out from under him? Get to the window, to Ludie and Jun at the window!

Ludie and Jun! She struggled to lift herself up, still clawing at the air above her. Gradually her heart stopped its hammering, slowing to a regular, even beat, like the tapping. Grady was gone, and only the hard, yellow light of the afternoon sun caressed her face. Marty rubbed her eyes awake, happiness and relief washing over her as reality returned.

She wasn't in the shed. She was in her bedroom at Aunt Letta's, where her mother had sent her to rest. The warm, bright bedroom with the familiar chintz curtains stirring slightly at the windows.

The windows claimed her attention now that she was fully awake, for the tapping, which she had thought to be part of her dream, continued, and she heard her name.

Sliding from the bed to the floor, she pattered over and pulled back the curtains.

The afternoon heat rushed at her face as Thad's big eyes and dark hair appeared.

"Oh, hey," she said sleepily. "I was sleeping. Mama made me."

"I heard you moving around and talkin'. I thought you might've waked up."

"I was just havin' a dream. What time is it, anyway?"

"I reckon 'bout four o'clock," he answered. "I just wanted to talk to you some, away from all them."

"What about?" Marty asked, yawning.

"Just some things." Thad kept his voice low, glancing toward the front of the house. "Can you come outside?"

"Well, yeah, but soon as Mama or Aunt Letta see me, they'll start jumping around and talking, and it might take a while."

"They're all on the front porch, drinking lemonade," said Thad. "Go through the kitchen and come on out back."

Within minutes Marty was tiptoeing across the back porch and down the steps. Thad stood beneath the big oak tree in the backyard, waiting. He motioned for her to follow him as he led the way to the grape arbor in his grandmother's backyard.

"I didn't mean to wake you up," he said when they were settled on the benches inside the leafy arch. "But I heard your mama say she was gonna get you up soon so you'd sleep tonight, and I didn't know if I'd get a chance to talk to you without all them being around."

Marty looked at the lush vines over her head. In a few weeks the powdery green clusters hanging there would be purple, sweet muscadines. "Well?" she asked, swatting at a bee. "What'd you want to talk about? If you're going to rub it in about how you told me not to take those pictures to Uncle Ray's store, and stay away from Ludie 'n all, I'm going right back over there." She still couldn't look him in the eye.

"I don't care about any of that." Thad plucked a green grape and rolled it around in his palm. "I mean I care, but that iddn't what I wanted to tell you."

"What then?"

"My mother . . ."

The image of the gracious lady loomed large in Marty's memory. "I know. If it hadn't been for her this morning, I don't know what would've happened. I thought about it later, and I never even got a chance to say thank you. She must think I'm awful."

"No, she don't," said Thad. "She said you remind her of herself when she was your age." He cleared his throat, then rose and stood with his back to Marty, looking out over the yard. "What I wanted to tell you is that I won't be down here anymore when you come. Mother wants me to stay in Chicago for good."

Marty didn't know what to say. She felt a little sad already at the prospect of visiting Caldwell and not having him for company, but also she was a bit envious of the exciting new life she was sure Thad was going to have in the big northern city of Chicago. "Do you want to go?"

He shrugged and turned back to her. "Kind of. It might be okay. I'd like it better if Bigmama would come too. She's the only one I care about down here."

Marty felt sorry for Thad. To spend your whole life in a place and not have a single friend you care about leaving.

"Mother said there's some boys my age in the apartment where they live that I might like."

He must have read her mind, she thought. "Well, if I were you, I'd be glad to get away from down here. With people like Jewel Turner and Grady Etheridge living here."

"How was it. Being kidnapped? Were you scared?"

"Well of course I was!" Was he crazy? "Scared to death at first. Then, after I knew they probably weren't going to hurt me, I was scared more for Chili. I thought one time they were going to hang him. Honest. They were talking about it!"

"Bigmama said your uncle Ray gave Cole Reid some money to drive Chili to a colored doctor in Augusta."

"I just hope Jewel and them get what they deserve for what they did. That's all I hope. Somebody ought to take a strap to them!" Marty snatched a leaf from the vine and began shredding it, watching the strips fall.

"Hunh," Thad grunted. "All they got was a good talkin' to. Mainly about gettin' you in on it. Nobody cares about Chili."

"No!" she cried. "After what they did?" Her eyes, her head, even her fingertips, burned with the current of sudden rage crackling through her. "They can't get away with—with just a—a talkin' to! You must've heard wrong!"

"Na-unh. I was in the swing over here on the front porch while you were asleep, and I heard Mr. Ray talking to your daddy about it. Even your daddy said it was probably more your fault, anyway, for stirring things up."

"It's not fair!" she wailed, feeling angry tears rise to her eyes. "It wasn't my fault that Chili got beaten up. It wasn't!" She wouldn't be the scapegoat for their cruelty! "And I'm going over there right now and tell 'em so!" Marty flew from the arbor, and was halfway across the yard when she heard Naomi call.

"Marty!"

Thad's mother came toward her, holding Marty fast with her large, compelling eyes.

Marty's narrow shoulders still heaved with the rapid breathing of rage, and her face was contorted, trying desperately to push back the tears slipping down her cheeks. She brushed them away fiercely. "What?" she sobbed, looking up into the elegant face of Naomi Walcott.

"Come back and sit down," said the older woman, taking Marty's arm and leading her back to the grape arbor.

The olive skin was taut across Naomi's high cheekbones, and the eyes, which matched the leaves behind her head, were serious as they gazed into Marty's. "I realize how upset you are, how unjust this all seems to you."

"It's not fair, Mrs. Walcott. After everything those boys did. It's not fair they should just get a tongue whipping!" Marty howled.

Long, soothing fingers, took Marty's hands. "I know, honey. But try to understand, if you can. Jewel and the others—well, they were only doing what they thought was expected of them."

"Expected of them? How can you say that?" Marty was feeling calmer with every stroke of the gentle fingers on her hand.

"It's true, Martha. Just as if they'd caught a fox in their father's chicken coop, they'd be expected to shoot it."

Marty was confused. She looked at Thad, who was frowning at his mother. "But what does that have to do with . . ."

Naomi released Marty's hands and stood up. She began pacing in front of them, rubbing her palms together under her chin. "I'm just trying to show you that those boys were just doing what they thought— what they have been taught—was right. And that is that when rules are broken, someone must pay."

"What rules were broken by me going to see Ludie?"

Naomi stopped and faced Marty. "You had a relationship with Ludie, and even if your association with Chili had not been misconstrued, well . . ." She inclined her head slightly, grimacing. "A friendship, a true, grown-up kind of friendship with a colored person is not acceptable."

Marty bit her lip, sighing deeply. "I guess I should have known from the first, when Chili told me to ask Aunt Letta if it'd be all right for me to visit with them."

"Yes," said Naomi, nodding sadly. "Chili knows the rules all too well."

"How come nobody ever wants to talk about these rules?" Thad asked.

"There's no way they can do that, son," she said, sitting next to him. Her face was suddenly so heavy with sorrow, it made Marty's eyes begin to mist over again. "Because if they did, if they talked about the rules," Naomi continued, "they would have to face the reality of how badly the Southern Negro had been treated all these years. That would be most unpleasant, and besides, there's no way of turning things around without upsetting our sacred Southern lifestyle. Worse still, if colored people should become our equals"—she hesitated, holding up her hand and turning it before them—"there is the danger of tainting that pure-white skin."

"Then the reason whites don't like coloreds is 'cause of their skin color?" asked Thad.

"Uncle Ray said it was because their brain was smaller, and if we mixed with them, it'd end up with nobody having any sense."

Naomi laughed, chasing the sorrow from her face. "Now come on, Marty. Do you really think Ludie's dumb?"

"Heavenly days, no! She's smart as all get-out."

"No," said Naomi. "That old myth about Negroes being stupid is just another brick in the great white wall of protection; dark skin, dark mind and all that. Color has always been the strongest threat." Naomi got up, stretching her arms to the top of the arbor. "I sometimes wonder," she said, pulling down a green tendril and winding it around her finger, "if the first slaves down here had been yellow, would the fear of contamination have been a shade less? Probably not," she said, tossing the bit of vine aside. "I didn't mean to get on my soapbox. You seemed about ready to storm the pearly gates there a while ago, Marty darling, and I was hoping to calm you down some." She took a few steps, then turned at the edge of the arbor. "One more thing, then I'm through." Naomi's eyes darted from Thad to Marty. "Try never to use anger as a weapon, because to be effective, a weapon must have an intellect behind it, not an emotion." She turned and walked away, the sunlight flashing patches of brightness through her dark hair.

Marty and Thad sat silently for a moment after his mother had gone. She didn't feel mad anymore, but she was a little sad. She wished the words she had so recently heard had come from her mother instead of Thad's.

She stood up, looking down at Thad. "Think I'll go get some lemonade. Want some?"

"I better not. Have to go see what books and games I want to take with me. When you going back to Augusta?"

Marty shrugged. "Tomorrow, I guess. When are you leaving?"

"Same. We have to go to Atlanta to get on the airplane."

"Look, Thad. Maybe you could write me a letter about Chicago when you get up there."

"Uh-huh." He began walking slowly toward his grandmother's house, and Marty turned toward her uncle's. "Marty." He spoke so low she could hardly hear him.

"What?"

"I . . . uh . . . well, I'm sorry all that stuff happened."

"Thanks, I know. I wish we were still little, having little biddy problems. Being punished for mud on my Sunday dress made me feel like this. 'Bye."

EIGHTEEN

My Lord, child, we thought you'd done been kidnapped all over again till your daddy spied you out the window talking to Thad." Her aunt put down her plate and came to Marty's side.

Moments before, Marty had come into the house through the back door, following the sound of her family's voices to the dining room. The oilcloth, which had covered the spread of food earlier, had been pulled back, and they sat on chairs, eating from plates in their laps.

"Are you hungry, darlin'?" asked her mother. "Want me to fix you a plate?"

"Not really, but I might eat a chicken leg and have some milk," Marty said, picking up a napkin and the chicken and going into the kitchen. When she had poured her milk, she looked up to see her mother standing beside her.

"Letta and Ray have the program at BTU tonight, so they have to go to church in a minute, but I was thinking . . . well, you haven't talked too much to your daddy and me about what happened, and if you feel like it, we'd like to hear."

Immediately Marty's mind began shutting doors, sealing off certain areas. "I guess so. If y'all want to. You already know most of it though." She took a swallow of milk. "I'm feeling better now. When are we going home?"

"Sometime tomorrow, I expect. Soon as Daddy is sure everything's been taken care of."

Before Marty could ask what "everything" was, Aunt Letta called.

"You want some of this cake, Martha, or some of Maybelle's pecan pie, before we put it all up?"

"Pie, please," answered Marty, walking back into the dining room.

George Armstrong was waving his fork at his brother. "He said hisself, military men don't make good presidents."

"Well, George," said Ray, "he haddn't been nominated yet, and he'll have to get by Stevenson even then. I hope this country's got more sense then to let them Republicans in, myself."

"I'll save you a place in the soup line, if Eisenhower does win."

Although the conversation around the table centered on politics, Marty knew from the way their eyes darted frequently to her that the events of the preceding night were uppermost in the minds of her family. She also knew that subjects of a personal nature, which might cause indigestion, were never discussed at mealtimes, and therefore she was safe for the moment. Not that she wanted to avoid talking about "what happened," as her mother had put it, but she was still disturbed by what Thad had said about her abductors going scot-free, and another emotional outburst was the last thing she wanted.

"Y'all go on, Letta. Martha and I'll take care of everything." Beth Armstrong began taking dishes to the kitchen.

"Speck we better, Ray," said Marty's aunt. "It's nearly five-thirty, and we ought to go over that material."

Most of the food had been put away, and Marty was stretching the elastic of a round plastic bowl cover over the dish of potato salad, before she spoke. "Mama, I'm real sorry you and Daddy had to interrupt your vacation just for me."

"Why, darlin', waddn't nothing else to do. Anyway

it waddn't entirely your fault." Her mother's hands were deep in the sink of suds, and she stared thoughtfully for a moment at a soapy plate in her hand. Then rinsing it and placing it aside to drain, she snatched up a towel, dried her hands, and faced Marty, scowling. "That's not altogether true. It was your fault." Marty watched as exasperation began to build on her mother's face. "It was every bit your fault, Martha Chafin. I know you had a bad night last night, but I have to agree with your daddy. You brought it all on yourself."

Marty opened her mouth, but her mother rushed on.

"Yes, you did. You had no business going over there to Ludie's, or Chili's, or whoever you said you went to see every day this week. You're nearly thirteen years old, and you've lived down here all your life. You know better than to do something like that." Beth Armstrong turned back to the sink with a weighty heave of her shoulders.

Outside Thad's dog was barking to come in, and the sun was having a last golden fling with the honeysuckle along the fence beside the house. Marty wiped the plate for the tenth time. "Why?" she asked.

Sloshing from the sink. "Why what?"

"Why wasn't . . . why *isn't* it all right to go to see Ludie? I like her. She's my friend!" Marty wondered if her mother would talk about "breaking the rules" as Naomi had done. She doubted it.

"Martha, you're talkin' crazy! You know good and well white people do not associate with nigrahs like that—like you did with that Ludie and her brother."

"I know that's what I've lived with, and what I've been told all my life, but I still don't know why it's wrong." She put the plate in an overhead cupboard and walked to the back door. "You let Sara fix my food, and when I was little she took care of me almost all the time, but yet if Sara had a daughter, I couldn't have her for a friend, like Anna Raye. Why, Mama?" Marty walked back to the sink and stared at the side of her mother's face until Beth Armstrong turned, a frown on her face and her blue eyes blinking, the way she always did when she was flustered.

"There's lots of reasons. Mostly, though, 'cause your backgrounds are so different, you have nothing in common!" Her mother dried her hands and folded her arms across the top of her apron, gazing at the refrigerator across the kitchen as if it contained the words she said next. "There're other reasons too. Yes, ma'am. Good reasons," she continued, nodding her head up and down, convincing herself. "For one thing, a girl like that wouldn't have all your advantages, all the pretty clothes you have, and she wouldn't understand why she couldn't do all the things you get to do."

"Then it would be just because she was poor that we couldn't be friends?"

Beth Armstrong put her hands to her face. The

blue eyes looked almost desperate, Marty thought. "I suppose. That's part of it. But Martha, it goes a lot deeper than money. Can't you see what I'm trying to say? You do. I can see by the look on your face, Martha Chafin, you've just got your head set in another direction. What's happened to you all of a sudden?" She was past frustration and on her way to anger again. Marty could tell. "Who in the world's been talkin' to you? I think I better go get your daddy. . . ." Her mother got as far as the door before Marty called to her.

"Not yet, Mama, please?"

Her mother stood in the doorway, her back to her, for several seconds. When she turned around, Marty saw that her eyes were moist, and round, with a kind of searching sadness. Beth Armstrong sat in a chair at the table, running her fingernail along its chrome border.

"Martha," she began, her voice steady. "I don't know how to talk to you about all of this, about the colored situation and all, because, well, in the first place, I never gave it much thought myself." The reddish fringe of her lashes played against her cheeks as she glanced from Marty to the action of her nail along the table's edge. "I know, though, that there're things happening in other parts of the country with regard to the nigrahs, and I'm not sure if they're right or wrong. All I do know is that down here, in the

South, the white-colored thing just isn't going to change. Not for a long, long time."

Marty rubbed her palms against her shorts several times, gathering her courage. "But do you think it's right, Mama? The way colored people can't go certain places and have to drink from different water fountains 'n all those kinds of things?"

"Right or wrong isn't what it's all about, Martha." Marty could feel her struggle across the table. "It's like asking if the air down here is right or wrong, or if it's right for the trees to bloom every year. It's just something that is. We don't have any control over it. Can't you see that? Oh, Lord," she said, sighing. "You've always been just about the most inquisitive child I've ever seen, but I never thought . . ." Her voice faced away.

Never mind, thought Marty. Just never mind, everybody. "Don't worry, Mama," she said, rising suddenly. "Probably has something to do with my age—starting my period 'n things. A stage I'm going through," she said with a shrug of her shoulders. "Just a stage, and I'll forget all about it when I get home." But even as she spoke the words, hoping to end her mother's unrest, Marty realized that the other voice, the one deep down, would never be still. Oh, it might have to speak softly for a few years, but somewhere, sometime later, it would be heard, and the questions it asked would find answers.

Beth Armstrong's eyes grew bright, as if a weight had been lifted from her. "Without a doubt, Martha Chafin," she said, surprise in her voice. "I don't know why I didn't think of that." She laughed, almost to herself. "Just a stage. The most natural thing in the world at your age. Come on. Let's go out on the porch with Daddy, darlin'."

For the next half hour Marty sat on the porch with her parents, telling them of her relationship with Sister, Chili, and Ludie. She tried to paint a picture of a normal family helping one another, living together, no different from her own. At first she had wanted merely to convince her parents that she had done nothing wrong in spending time with such a family. Then, before she realized it, she was telling them about Ludie, hoping they would see her through her eyes: an intelligent, sensitive young woman, with a gift to share with the world. She still had not given up the idea of helping Ludie with her art.

"You really should see some of Ludie's good pictures."

"Are they the ones you lied about? The ones you said you drew?" her father said accusingly.

"Oh, Daddy," she said with a sigh. He hadn't heard a word she'd said for the last half hour. "I just thought that was the only way for people to see Ludie's art. Then, when they saw how great the pictures were, it wouldn't matter who drew them."

"Well, you're wrong about that. It does matter."

Her father's face was stern. "She's still a nigger, and no self-respecting white person is gonna have any kind of nigger doings of that nature in his home. May as well have a big picture of that Booker T. Washington or George Washington Carver hanging in a place of honor. It'll never happen!"

"Miz Rountree already did," Marty said softly.

"What'd you say?" her father asked loudly.

"I said, Daddy, that Miz Rountree already bought one of Ludie's pictures that was in Uncle Ray's store." She was trying not to get angry. "She thought it was wonderful and had it framed, and everything. It's hanging in her livingroom right now." She couldn't help herself. Her chin was high in defiance of her parents.

"No, it iddn't, Martha," said her mother quietly beside her.

"Yes, it is. Aunt Letta told me."

"Your mama's right. You put your uncle Ray in a bad situation with those people. He felt like the only decent thing to do was to explain to the Rountrees who actually did that picture. Naturally they returned it. Ray's bringing the others back from the store."

She couldn't believe what she was hearing. Fury, her constant companion lately, pounded inside her, throbbing with each suppressed idea of retaliation. Suppressed, because she was remembering what Naomi had said about anger being a useless weapon. No. She would wait. Presently her breathing became calmer and she began to move her chair back and forth in a carefully metered rocking movement. She was glad she hadn't talked back to her father. Her words weren't ready. Her ideas not entirely complete. But they would be. And soon.

As soon as her uncle came around the front of the car, Marty saw the pictures. Rolls of brown paper, carefully tied with white string on either end. Why had he bothered? Why hadn't he just wadded them up and flung them across the woods to Ludie?

Her uncle's eyes were on Marty's face as he mounted the porch steps with the pictures. "We have to see Ludie gets these back tomorrow." It wasn't his words so much as how he had sounded when he spoke them that gave Marty the feeling that her uncle was sorry about something.

She got up and followed him into the house, watching as he laid the pictures aside and sat down in his chair. She sat, too, on the ottoman at his feet, peering up into his face. "Uncle Ray, Ludie is a good artist, don't you think?"

"Yes, ma'am, Martha," said Aunt Letta from the doorway. "As good as ever I saw."

"But because she's colored," Marty continued, "the Rountrees and others don't want her pictures? Is that it?"

Her uncle nodded, but didn't speak.

"Uncle Ray, is Ludie a child of God?"

She heard her aunt's sharp intake of breath.

Uncle Ray ducked his head, staring hard at the arms of the chair. "Don't start, Martha."

"But Uncle Ray, didn't you tell me we ought to treat everybody the same, rich or poor, clean or dirty." She paused. "Colored or white?"

His brown eyes rolled upward and he shook his head, then went to stand beside the front window. "Little gal, you sho' have thrown a monkey wrench into things this week. I'll say that."

The *ribbling* of the rockers on the porch stopped, and Marty knew her parents were listening through the open window.

"I guess Jesus must have thrown the monkey wrench, Uncle Ray, long time ago, when he told us to 'do unto others as we would have them do unto us.' I just realized this week that colored people are 'others' too."

"You're too young to understand it all, Martha," he said, his back to her.

"I don't think so, Ray," said her aunt. "I think she understands . . . everything."

When she came into the kitchen the next morning, Marty was surprised to see her uncle Ray sitting at the table with her parents.

"I don't see the necessity of getting into all this, Ray," her father was saying.

"George, it's not a question of something that's necessary." He stopped as Marty sat down. "Good morning, missy. Bet you slept better last night than you did the night before."

"I did, and I'm hungry too." She looked toward the stove, where Thelma was dishing up sausage and eggs. "What time are we leaving today, Daddy?"

"In a bit. Your mama wants a piece of ham from the store."

"Is Ludie coming to get the linen today?" she asked, her eyes darting from face to face to catch some reaction.

"Yes, she is," said her mother. "And you can say good-bye to her if you want to."

"You can also hear what Uncle Ray's gon' say to her, too, when she gets here." Aunt Letta was glowing like she'd hidden the egg again.

"Don't worry," said her uncle. "It's nothing bad. In fact, it's what you wanted all along."

"You're going to put her pictures back in the store?" asked Marty excitedly.

Across the table her uncle's palms flew up. "Now wait a minute. I just can't do that right now. What I am going to do is try to help her get started with her artwork. Get her some decent drawing tools and all. See about getting her somewhere to a good art teacher. That's all. The rest'll be up to Ludie."

Marty leaped up and flew to her uncle, throwing her arms around him. "Oh, Uncle Ray . . . Uncle Ray. You're wonderful. You'll see! She'll be even better than she is now. She'll gets lots of money, maybe have an operation, and—"

"Don't go gettin' your hopes up, Martha, about this," interrupted her father. "There's a lot of details to be worked out, and you should be thankful your uncle's willing to help somebody like Ludie."

"Your daddy's right about details," said Uncle Ray. "Remember, too, I still got to live in Caldwell and make a living. It wouldn't do for it to get out that I'm taking on anything like this, but well, you started us all to thinking last night. Then, later, Letta and I walked over and talked to Naomi. She said she'd do all she could to help, once Ludie got going, even find a place for her up North if it came to that. Remember, though, it's got to be a secret for the time being."

Marty began to swirl about the kitchen. "I will! I'll keep the secret, but just think! Ludie'll have a chance now! At least she'll have that!"

The sound came from far away at first. Marty stopped, inclining her head toward the front of the house. There it was again. "Yanh, yanh, yan, ee, ee, yanh."

It was the same haunting strain that had made her heart pound with fear only one week ago, wafting up the lane and through the trees, causing her heart to pound once more. But not with fear. Not this morning. Oh no! This morning it beat with joy—happy, hopeful joy!

Ludie's Song

Marty ran through the house and out to the front porch. The bent figure was shuffling up the lane toward the house. Marty jumped to the sun-spattered ground beneath the trees; down the grassy bank and across the dusty red road she ran, her arms outstretched toward Ludie, toward her friend. "Ludie . . . Ludie," she called, waving her arms.

The blue kerchief nodded, and Marty knew Ludie was smiling her crooked smile. "Yanh . . . yan . . ."

Soon, Ludie, your words may be different. Oh yes, Ludie, someday soon your song will be new! Perhaps the whole world will hear . . . Ludie's song!

ABOUT THE AUTHOR

Dirlie Herlihy was born in Portsmouth, Virginia, and grew up in Macon, Georgia. She studied theater arts at Mercer University in Macon, and creative writing at the University of North Florida in Jacksonville. She has written for local radio and television, but *Ludie's Song* is her first novel. Ms. Herlihy lives in Advance, North Carolina, with her husband, James Gordon Herlihy. They have three grown children.